NUMBER TWELVE IN THE SYBIL NORCROFT SERIES

WAR AND THE END GAME

Incumbent President Sybil Norcroft

BY
CARL DOUGLASS

Neurosurgeon turned Author writes with
Gripping Realism

PUBLICATION
CONSULTANTS
We Believe In The Power Of Authors

PO Box 221974 Anchorage, Alaska 99522-1974
books@publicationconsultants.com—www.publicationconsultants.com

ISBN Number: 978-1-63747-124-1
eBook ISBN Number: 978-1-63747-125-8

Library of Congress Number: 2022951655

Manufactured in the United States of America

DISCLAIMER

All the eight novellas in the McGee Series are works of fiction and should not be construed as representing real persons, places, or events. Some names of real persons and places appear but only for the purpose of creating a setting in the real world or as a mention of historical circumstances. None of the real people or the real places were actually involved in the fictional portrayals found in these short books.

DEDICATION

To everyone who despises human traffickingand does something about it.

CHAPTER
ONE

Lincoln Howard and his hand-picked team of assassins entered North Korea via a HALO [High Altitude, Low Opening] parachute jump into the deeply forested north country near the border with China. They had practiced doing HALOs endlessly, and the landing was accomplished without a hitch. The usual SEAL team platoon consists of sixteen men (and the rare woman), and Lincoln's intelligence paramilitary unit was organized in the same way: two officers, one chief, and thirteen enlisted men, although it was not actually a military platoon. The members had extensive military special ops backgrounds; so, the SEAL type organization was comfortable for them. They were all specially selected for Lincoln's unit: every man–and their one woman–had taken out at least three persons in direct hand-to-hand killing—including ambushes, surprise fights while on duty, and long-distance exterminations. Twelve members were certified snipers, and all could shoot at least at the marksman level, the majority at the sharpshooter level, and a decent minority at the expert level, with both handgun and rifle.

Firearms and other lethal weapons training was most exacting, and the product turned out by the long experience and specific training made the US assassin group the best of the best in the world of black operators. Every man trained and tested in NRA Precision Pistol–conventional pistol shooting, is a bullseye shooting competition where three handguns of differing calibers are used.

Competency in High Power Rifle–Across the Course—required each man to shoot Across the Course—in which each man shoots 3-position (standing, kneeling, or sitting, and prone) at 200, 300, and 600 yards; Field-Shooting–Terrain-Shooting—is a set of pistol and rifle shooting that includes temporary shooting ranges in the terrain at varying and unknown distances; PRS [Precision Rifle Series] combines field and long range shooting disciplines where rifles with battle rifle cartridges are shot on irregular terrain at varying distances from about 10 to 1000 meters; CISM Rapid Fire match is a sped-up version of the ISSF 300 m Standard Rifle and handgun shooting; running target shooting which involved a shooting target—sometimes called a boar, moose, or deer—that was made to move as if it were a running animal or to disappear unexpectedly; and finally, clay pigeon shotgun shooting at flying clay pigeon targets. The elites in Lincoln Howard's tightly knit group had to achieve sharpshooter level twice out of four yearly reevaluations.

They trained constantly; but once a year, they had to pass a do-or-die grueling shooting test that–like Navy

SEAL training—would eliminate the majority of lesser men. The assassins had to endure two day-long tests in any kind of weather that existed those days that evaluated their competence with multi-gun use and transition. The tests were practical shooting events where each of the men and women used—in rapid changes–a combination of rifles, handguns, and shotguns; long range shooting at such distances that sight adjustment based from judging atmospherically present or changing conditions became critical and mimicked real combat conditions as near as possible.

Each shooter was required to fire a minimum 140 rounds in at least twelve individual stages, over the course of the two exhausting days at targets located 100, 500, 800, 1000, and 1500 meters. To qualify as a sniper, the shooter had to be able to hit a man-sized target at one and two miles with 50% accuracy three out of five tries. Only four of Howard's snipers qualified as "experts", and he was one of them—no pressure on him, of course.

None of the elite corps members could rest on the laurels gained as civilians or military members, however superb. Being a roving assassin in the most secret, and most effective, unit in the pay of the US government, meant starting over to be able use their skills for a new kind of service. First, they underwent rigorous psychological evaluations and repeated them quarterly during their term of service. Second, they had the best trainers in all sorts of combat: mano-a-mano with hard fists, stiff fingers, elbows, knees, feet, and heads. The disciplines included Jiu Jitsu with Pedro Sauer—the small and completely effective trickster; Silat for street fighting, by Burton Richardson;

Kung Fu by Wang Bo, formerly of Shaolin Temple; Kenpo Karate by Tony Martinez Sr., who received his black belt from Ed Parker and Mills Crenshaw—two of the toughest and most down-to-earth teachers of fighters who ever lived; and Krav Maga which is the free flowing self-defense and combat attack training required of IDF soldiers and all Mossad agents. It is eclectic and employs all styles of punching, kicking, chokes, take-downs, with the aim of neutralizing the enemy in the shortest amount of time and in the most effective way possible. It is based on courage, strength, speed, precision, and lethality.

The last—and for many—the most difficult training to achieve good marks in were knife throwing and crossbow shooting at varying distances and with both stationary and moving targets.

The transport flight to their LDZ [landing zone] in Manchuria was predetermined by on-the-ground CIA agents and their operative assets. The departure time from The Farm in Virginia was timed to put them into their parachutes in the middle of the darkest part of the night—popularly called "O dark-thirty".

Manchuria is a region in East Asia. For the purposes of Howard's unit, it was defined as a region divided between Northeast China and the Russian Far East–the Russian part known as Outer Manchuria, and the Chinese part as Inner Manchuria. Manchuria is delimited by the Yablonoi range in the north, the Greater Khingan in the west, and the Pacific coast [the Japanese or East Sea] in the east. In the south it is delimited from the Korean peninsula by the Yalu River its entire length. The river's origin is Paektu Mountain on the China–North Korea border from which it flows south to Hyesan before sweeping 130 km northwest to Linjiang and then returning to a more southerly route for a further 300 km to empty into the Korea Bay at Dandong, China.

At the exact GPS coordinates–42°33′N 129°01′E–the sixteen well-trained, well-supplied, and anxious, killers, HALO parachuted into a small open grassland surrounded by otherwise heavily wooded virgin forested mountain terrain sixty km from the Yalu river, and nearly 100 km from where they had to cross the Yalu into the secretive and extremely security conscious North Korea. They were less than twenty klicks from Helong in the northern Chinese province of Jilin.

The Americans were wearing night vision goggles and were able to see well enough to work. They quickly and efficiently carried their parachutes to the trees surrounding the open grassy area and buried them three feet deep in the rich black soil of Manchuria. Using their cricket clickers, all men were quickly accounted for. The jump had gone off without a hitch.

They lay down in the tall grass just inside the sight barrier of the trees and waited half an hour. A large farm truck without shining its headlights rumbled into the center of the open area. Lincoln flashed his light three times on, three off and was greeted by the same sign.

"Throw your gear on, and let's mount up," he said.

In twenty minutes, every man and his gear were aboard the renovated truck bed which provided ample room for the men and equipment but lacked even rudimentary provision for comfort. Their destination was the border checkpoint at the foot of a new bridge connecting the northeastern Chinese city of Jian with North Korea's city of Manpo. The good thing about that choice was that it was relatively close, and the China-DPRK Jian-Manpo highway connection was decent for passenger and cargo transport. The crossing point hosted an advanced and comfortable customs facility. The bad thing about that choice was the same as the good things because they would be in plain sight as long as they were on the highway.

That shortcoming required that they travel only at night, which slowed progress. They had a choice to wade across the river at a different point above the new bridge where the Yalu River was only about three feet deep which would require leaving behind a considerable amount of their heavy equipment, or to cross the bridge hidden under boxes and tarpaulins during daylight hours, the only time the customs station was open. They debated the choice as the truck moved relatively swiftly south on the highway. They decided to chance crossing via the bridge, even though it could mean a shoot-out and destroying their element of secrecy and surprise for the rest of their journey.

The CIA agent who had procured the truck and knew the area very well was a North Korean defector. That meant that he spoke the local dialect like a native—which was true. He assured them that security with regards to transport trucks was quite lax, because there were so few crossings; and the commerce between the PRC and the DPRK had increased exponentially during the past five or so years that it was imperative to keep traffic moving.

For all its discomforts, the arrangements in the bed were ingenious enough to make up for the aches and pains. They were hidden in a copse of trees as daylight approached. The sixteen US agents ate their morning ration of peanut butter, ravioli, freeze-dried curry, and bubblegum. Bad as it was, breakfast was an improvement over the kelp jerky they had for supper. Their CIA agent—the man with no name—had only a limited supply of MREs and some Mountain House LRPs left over from the war in Viet Nam. The agents for whom he was responsible would have to make do until they could get near a city where they could steal decent food.

The male agents lay out on the floor of the truck bed arranged transversely like so many logs. Empty cardboard boxes were neatly placed over them, and finally a tarp covered the bed and was lashed to the sides. The air was dank and odoriferous—smelled of the manure of the thousands of domestic animals that had been hauled there over the years, and of the blood of animals being taken from the slaughter houses.

"There's a court martial waiting for any one of you who coughs, sneezes, hiccoughs, or moans. Am I understood?"

There was a mumbled acquiescence.

As predicted, the customs station was sparsely manned in the early morning hours immediately after it opened. Chinese agents on the Jilin side, and North Korean agents on the Manpo, northwestern Chagang Province side were sleepy, hung over from their previous evening's partying, and lacked energy to open the tarp. With a little grunting and grumbling, the driver and his "wife"–the lone woman

11

among the American agents–had a cursory check of their papers. She—like the driver—was a diminutive defector from the army from southern North Korea; so, her accent was off some. She said as little as possible.

The highway to Manpo was not nearly as well maintained as that on the Chinese side, and the ride produced considerably more minor bruises and joint pains. The driver found an out-of-the-way alley where he could stop and allow the US agents to get out and stretch their sore joints and muscles. They were in the medium size town of Manpo along the shores of the Yalu River so close to China that they could see Ji'an, Jilin province, PRC. Their next destination was Camp 7 Hoeryong North Hamgyong Province on the banks of the Yalu.

As they drove up the main highway to Hamgyong Province, Lincoln explained their target–a camp commandant named General Shin Ahn Chol-hwan— who was listed on the United Nations most wanted list.

"The man was sent by Chairman Kim to restore order after a family of five attempted to escape, was caught, and torture murdered, in a public execution. A riot ensued, and nearly 2,000 prisoners were sent to the detention center where they were savagely tortured, then taken to the execution site in Sugol Valley, at the edge of the camp. Two escapees reported to South Korean authorities that they saw saw disfigured and crushed bodies, one of whom was the father of the family who attempted to escape and brought on the riots and the horrific punishments. General Shin personally oversaw the punishments—a privilege granted him because he was a cousin by marriage of the ruling Kim family.

"He is a confidant of the Dear Leader's and is reportedly going to be promoted to the inner circle of Kim's generals. Apparently, Kim holds the man in high esteem, hence, he is one of our chief targets."

The closer they drew to the *kwan-li-seo* [Camp 7 Hoeryong large political prisoner labor colony]—officially known as Maximum Security Area Kwalliso Penal Labor Colony No. 22–the less traffic they encountered. The camp was a maximum-security area, completely isolated from the outside world. They successfully passed through the first checkpoint, but the scrutiny was so severe that Lincoln and the CIA agent driver decided that they would likely not survive another security post encounter.

They hid their truck in a ramshackle and abandoned junk yard, collected what they needed, and hid out in the nearby forest until dark. The camp itself was—like many others—located in a secluded mountain valley completely isolated from the outside world; the total number of prisoners held in the central and northeastern regions of the DPRK was estimated by CIA operatives to be 150,000 to 200,000, with nearly 50,000 wretched souls doomed to live out their entire lives in the camp. The North Korean government denied Camp 7/22's existence.

Each agent carried a crisp, clear color photograph of Gen. Shin. The camp was situated in a large valley with many side gullies, gulches, and valleys, surrounded by fairly high mountains—very similar to the terrain in which the agents had trained. The main gate was actually located in Kaishantun, China and was the most heavily guarded. The southwest gate of the camp was located only seven km from downtown Hoeryong, making it the most desirable for the assassins to breach. The camp was not included in maps, and the North Korean government denied its existence.

Finding a way in was not going to be easy. CIA and DOD engineers estimated that the camp was 225 km^2 in area and surrounded by a double fence the entire perimeter. The inner was a 3,300 volt electric fence and the outer a coiled razor wire barrier. The security officers of the DPRK put devilish traps and hidden nails between the two fences. The security was controlled by just over 1,000 guards and 600 administrative agents, all under the direction of General Shin Ahn Chol-hwan. The guards were equipped with automatic rifles, hand grenades, and vicious trained dogs. The WOMs [Wise Old Men] in Washington did not have a plan for getting into the camp, much less any suggestions as to how to get near the general.

The driver—Park Do Yoon, his name still an official secret—had been to the Hoeryong and Camp 7/22 area several times and had served there as a prisoner for six years before escaping. He had memorized a rough map of the camp and made a point to learn all he could about the headquarters building where Gen. Shin spent most of his time. The most valuable thing he kept in his memory bank was the location of an escape site through a section of fence near the Tumen River, which formed the border with China.

During the night, the unit force marched from the outskirts of Hoeryong towards the confluence of the Yalu and Tumen Rivers. The location of the opening through— more precisely, under—the devil's fence was indelibly emblazoned in Do Yoon's brain because he had discovered how and where to create it and had assisted twelve other escapees over the past seven years.

In the dark, all the fence line the agents could make out looked the same as everywhere else.

"We are here," Do Yoon announced after a two-hour fast walk.

The place looked no different than any stretch north or south, that Lincoln's agents could see.

"You doubt me, Great Spies? Allow me to demonstrate."

Do Yoon walked quietly up to the fence line and began moving some loose brush and trash from the bottom of the fence. Every agent was surprised to see that there was a stretch of the bottom of the fence that did not enter deep into the earth, as the fence did in other areas they had tested. He moved two inches of loose dirt to clear an area of four feet square, under which was a flat, sturdy wooden lid.

"Please to run your hand along the edges of the door and feel for a ring."

Do Yoon did the same as the Lincoln's CIA officer. He found the large ring first and pulled on it with all his strength. The door lifted up to reveal a large box. With considerable effort Do Yoon and Patrick Spencer forced the door upwards and moved the lower border of the double fence up with it. There was enough for a man and a half with his backpack in place to slide into the sturdy open top base and through to the inside of the *kwan-li-seo*.

"We go to the *Haengyong-ri* now [the camp headquarters with administration offices, a food factory, a garment factory, detention center, guards› quarters, and prisoner family quarters.]," Do Yong said softly.

"Not to make noise. Guards and their dogs come with no regular schedule. Last man through replace the junk on outside of fence. This place is the most important secret in the world for the poor people inside. I tell only to a very selected few.

"Following me. No noise. Tie metal things to body; so, no clanking is heard by the enemy."

The night was inky black which was cut only a little by night vision goggles. The seventeen people moved slowly over the uneven ground, each person holding the right shoulder of the person ahead of him or her. Lincoln calculated that they had gone somewhere between two or three klicks before Do Yong called an abrupt halt.

"This is the place where the monster sleeps," he said flatly.

Lincoln extended his left arm and was astonished to contact a brick wall that he could not see, even then.

"Amazing, my friend," he said. "We are going to call you 'spider' because you have such great eyes."

"Good, I like to be a spider. Follow me," he said, then quoted, 'said the spider to the fly'."

Lincoln mentally kicked himself for not remembering that he had been informed that the CIA operative had been educated in American universities. He laughed and got a little chuckle of pride from Do Yong.

"It is time to do the deed," Do Yong whispered as he started walking unerringly towards the sumptuous bed room of General Shin Ahn Chol-hwan.

CHAPTER
TWO

There is an oddity–or perhaps better described as arrogance–that the security forces manning the guard posts and perimeters of Camp 22 were far more intent on preventing any escapes. An escape of a detainee with the subsequent communication to the interested public of the western world would mean that heads would roll, and that there would be a new commandant chosen—as a consequence of the untimely death of the current holder of that dubious title. A further consequence of the arrogant hyperattention to the issue of escape was a very limited interest in security for the guards themselves or even the commandant, General Shin Ahn Chol-hwan.

Lincoln Howard and his assassins maneuvered to fill that void of apathetic disinterest. In the dark of night, they separated and crept surreptitiously and silently to the general' headquarters and personal quarters—the *Haengyong-ri*–which he shared with his wife, seven children, and—in a separate apartment–a very attractive young mistress. The killers reunited at a rear entrance which had no guards, and the door was not even locked. There had been only one casualty during the approach— one young and unsuspecting guard—enjoying his last smoke—was felled by a steel arrow from a crossbow. The arrow was removed, and the corpse was dragged off into the nearby trees.

Once inside the opulent residential section of the headquarters building, the assassins again separated and took four different routes to the general's bedroom, a place known from his menial cleaning work assignments by Do Yoon. Another two security guards perished, this time from broken necks and severed cervical spinal cords as the assassins closed in on the finely appointed bed-room.

Lincoln put his finger to his lips and tried the door latch to the bedroom. It opened with silent ease. Lincoln and two of his men crept inside, aided by their soft soled boots pressing into the plush, deep pile, wall-to-wall, English wool carpet. The general was alone in the palatial room, and the only sound was his post drunken snoring.

The two associates assumed security positions. Lincoln poured enough chloroform to moisten a soft cloth and stopped Gen. Shin's obnoxious snoring and calmed the intense halitosis of his mouth-open breathing. Then, Lincoln and one of his men turned the general over on his left side and flexed his neck to its limit. Then Lincoln extracted an ice pick from his back-pack and expertly inserted it between the man's lower occipital bone and first cervical vertebra and into his posterior fossa. A few circular motions of the ice-pick into the man's medulla oblongata resulted in his respirations, heart-beat, and pulse stopping. The entire killing was done in complete silence.

Do Yong had made a request–his only one for all of his services—"SAC [Special Agent in Charge], in my mind, it would be good to remove the general's body and take it to the execution site in Sugol Valley and impale him on a post—the way he handled such things."

Another agent added to that suggestion, "And, we should break him up with the sledge-hammers he has handy over there."

A third inventive agent thought up another useful tactic, "I think we should steal every valuable small thing in this room to confuse Uncle Kim's investigators. They are going to be inclined to blame the guards and the detainees and overlook how our activities in the name of Uncle Sugar might possibly have contributed."

Lincoln did not hesitate. He smiled and gave a quick, "yes" to all three suggestions.

As they were preparing to board the truck again to make their escape, Clyde Draper–the agent who made the suggestion about the hammers—took a moment to ask Lincoln a question.

"Boss, did we just commit a first-degree murder?"

"Define 'murder', "Lincoln said in answer.

Clyde gave it some thought, then said, "The illegal taking the life of a human being, I suppose."

"And the Ten Commandments says it more simply, 'Thou shalt not kill.'"

"Too simple; to take that literally would mean there could be no killing animals to eat, or insects to get rid of pests, or righteous judicial executions, or self-defense or defense of home and family, or soldiers acting under time of war."

"All right, I take it that you basically approve of the list you cited."

"Yeah, I guess so."

"Do you see our actions as coming under any one of those rubrics, Clyde?"

Clyde pondered for a long moment an answered just as it was time to board, "I see where you're going with this, but, I guess that my issue when you get right down to it, is will I be able to face my Maker on Judgment Day?"

Lincoln's last rejoinder was, "Clyde, I don't believe in any of those religious superstitions; but since you seem to, then hold your head up high and look the Diety in the eye and tell Him or Her that you have no repenting to do related to your actions in this killing or the others we have had to do for King and Country. They were righteous."

True to expectations, there were no news items regarding either the deaths in northern North Korea or even the existence of the place of the deaths within the country or outside its borders. No one paid the lumbering old truck any attention as they traveled south on the new Hunchun–Ulanhot Expressway [commonly referred to as the *Hunwu Expressway*] to Najin in Rason, Province on the east (Pacific) coast of Iran. There was little to distinguish the humble place other than that it was a year-round ice-free port, and nothing to draw tourists from anywhere except a small facility–the Rason Emperor Hotel and

Casino–a resort and casino owned by the Emperor Group, a diversified Hong Kong based commercial group–that catered almost entirely to Chinese. Its population was 66,000 and it was situated at elevation nine meters above sea level.

Chin Yu-en Lee was sent by the PRC to handle the powerful neighbor's banking needs developing in the North Korean port city. China is making investments in the port as it gives it access to the Sea of Japan. The DPRK allowed China's domestic trade cargo to be shipped via its port in Najin from northeast to east China. Coal was shipped from nearby Chinese mines to Shanghai—an altogether cozy relationship for both countries–especially for the economically struggling North Korea. Lincoln Howard and his agents were sent by the DNI and DCIA to Najin expressly to deal with the threat Chin Yu-en Lee posed to the United States.

It was enough to come to the attention of Lincoln and his assassinations that Chin was considered to be part of the inner circle of Kim Jong Un, but that he was probably the most well-informed and friendly banker for the Hermit Kingdom. He held financial records well known to his masters–the leaders in Beijing–but only vaguely known to Kim and his government. Chin had maneuvered himself into the position of being irreplaceable for the Dear Leader. The PRC had used considerable of its leverage to put the small, but powerful man into his extraordinarily important position.

The Korean People's Navy maintained a naval training base at the Rajin Port in the city of Rason. In addition,

Rason was home to No. 28 Shipyard Najin. The yard was highly profitable since it had an exclusive contract to be a principle shipbuilder and supplier to the Korean People's Navy. Chin Yu-en Lee was the owner of record of a Chinese company named Chin Maritime Enterprises that held the Najin shipyard lease for ten years at the port. Fifty percent of all funding for and profits from the enterprise emanated from and returned to General Secretary of the CPC and the president of the PRC, Xi Jinping personally. Mr. Chin was a very important person in a strategic position, and that made him continually suspect and always necessarily on guard.

Unfortunately for Mr. Chin, he was a man of obsessive regularity; and the CIA could recite verbatim every stop and for how long, the important banker made on any given day. This day, he was going to have lunch with *Sojang* [Rear Admiral] Park Ji-hu to finalize the appropriations necessary for the final phase of the Rajin Port. As always, the two men met in the best restaurant in Rason–the Rason Emperor Hotel and Casino Sino-Korean Buffet–an outdoor bar and grill featuring the best-of-the-best mixed crab luncheon.

Adm Park had a gambling problem. In fact, Chin owned the man because he paid off a gambling debt that the admiral had so foolishly allowed to accumulate that he had lost an amount in excess of his entire yearly salary, and a considerable dip into PRC funding for the Rajin Naval Academy's next fiscal year, a crime for which he would have been hanged had it become known.

After the excessive meal, and the formality of Adm Park signing off on every item Chin requested and from which he would profit at close to seventy-five percent, the admiral checked his pocket and was pleased to find that he had more than three thousand €, far in excess of the exorbitant entry fee of five hundred €. The two men shook hands, bowed; and the admiral took his leave for the casino and an afternoon of unfettered gambling.

Mr. Chin luxuriated in his current success with a flute from his celebratory 750 ml. bottle of 2008 sparkling Louis Roederer Cristal Brut from Champagne, France and a pungent Cuban Cohiba cigar. He closed his eyes, tilted his head back to have a quick power nap, and died of a GSW to the head from a Russian 7.62x54R—SV Dragunov Sniper Rifle which fired a 7N14 armor-piercing sniper round [152gr at ~2750fps].

Pandemonium reigned in the outdoor grill with rich Chinese and North Koreans diving for cover under every heavy chair and table. No shooter was ever sighted. No amount of investigation ever turned up a motive or a name. Why any Russian would want a North Korean minor businessman dead defied reason. The governments of the city of Rajin, the province of Rason, the leadership of North Korea, and the PRC, preferred to handle the incident in such a way that it was never described in print or seen on television. It never happened.

Enjoying the success of taking out the first two targets, Lincoln and his team made two significant decisions. The first was in direct accordance with orders and plans hatched by the WOMs to divide into five separate smaller groups to go after five targets at once. The reasoning was that the group of sixteen Americans would draw too much attention, and the targets were fairly wide-spread and considered to be softer targets that the previous two. The second decision was to utilize single assassins for three of the targets because one person would have easier access than would a team. The latter decision was fraught with more hazard than the other plans. It was going to have to include actual North Koreans as the up-close-and-personal hit men and women.

The issue was not finding citizens of the Hermit Kingdom who hated enough and for good enough reason to be able to gather the courage and determination to go through with a killing, but being able to find haters capable enough and who could be adequately trained.

This was very likely to turn out to be the most time-consuming venture of the several remaining to accomplish. Lincoln and the rest of the team unanimously agreed that the most likely success would come from utilizing the only woman on the team–So-Hui Namkuhng–for the removal of a secretive nuclear engineer who lived in Myŏngch'ŏn. The WOMs had stressed the vital importance of the targeted man, who was one of the most determined hawks among the nuclear scientists and considered by the French to be the most brilliant and creative.

Namkuhng—whose given name was unpronounceable by her comrades—ended up being called simply "Nam"—was very small, even by North Korean standards. She was a native of Pyongyang and had been trained since she was a child in all the arts of assassination. She was far stronger than she looked, far quicker than anyone expected, and the third best martial artist—male or female–in the country from the time she was twelve—and outclassed every woman who had ever been part of the RGB [Reconnaissance General Bureau, officially the Reconnaissance Bureau of the General Staff Department].

The RGB is the highly respected and feared intelligence agency that manages the state›s clandestine operations. Most of their operations have a specific focus on Japan, South Korea, and the United States. She was originally assigned to work in Japan; and there besides killing critics of the regime, she became secretly enamored with democracy and capitalism. That assignment put her into contact with American intelligence personnel; and to make a long story short, she was able to defect to the US. The DPRK had its suspicions but was never able to be certain what had happened to one of their best agents and assassins.

Her Korean accent was a bit tainted by her long stay in Japan, but it was not so far off that people would draw the conclusion that she was of South Korean origin. She was delighted to get the assignment; so, she could prove her worth to her teams and to the WOMs. Her resolve had been fixed when she saw the poor wretches in Camp 22. She felt a sincere need to repent for what she had done to further such treatment of other human beings when she was part of the North Korean army, even though she had had no real choice in the matter. Working with Lincoln Howard's unit was a way back for her.

It was necessary for Nam to have at least two others along for her mission. One reason was that they had to carry some heavy boxes. The other was to have a backup if things went wrong. The choice of whom to send with her was perplexing since the unit had no Koreans other than Nam. Lincoln settled on his two Latinos, Miguel Rodriguez-Lopez and Pedro Lobos.

Abe Costner, the most outspoken member of the unit, asked, "Boss… really, do you think Miguel and Pedro can pass?"

"We'll have to make them as 'passable' as possible. A little change of haircut, big field hats, the right clothes, and put them in a big crowd. I think it will work. It has to."

"I don't know boss, seems to me like we're painting a sign on their backs, 'US SPY'."

"Have some optimism, Abe. They'll look like downtrodden field hands to anyone who takes a look from fifty meters while riding by on a galloping horse."

Abe had to laugh, and even Nam thought it was funny. But she was a 'make-do' sort of person, and that was exactly what she intended to do.

The three members of the Myŏngch'ŏn assassination squad stole a suitable looking old farm truck from an old rice farmer who apparently was too old to use it any longer and puttered their way toward Myŏngch'ŏn *Kun* [County] in North Hamgyong province located near the center of the country. An intermediate-range ballistic missile base was located there, and a mandatory-attendance parade to honor the Highest Person was scheduled for the following day. All three members of the unit had full face color photos of their quarry, Nuclear Engineer Bora Nahn. He was likely to stand out because he was a rare Korean official who had enough facial hair to go about with a full-face black beard.

CHAPTER
THREE

The parade in Myŏngch'ŏn was slated to begin in fifteen minutes. So-Hui Namkuhng, Miguel Rodriguez-Lopez, and Pedro Lobos rushed through the nearly empty outskirts roads towards the Musudan intermediate-range ballistic missile base. As they drew closer the crowds were ever more numerous and trying to move more rapidly in order to avoid being late for the beginning of the important gathering. A rumor had started and gathered wildfire intensity that the Superior Person himself was going to be present. Everyone carried a mobile; so, they could at least prove that they were in attendance. A selfie with the Dear Respected Comrade Leader in the background would be proof-positive.

The Americans could get their truck no closer than two klicks from the area where the parade was to end and the speeches were to begin. Engineer Bora Nahn was to give the opening speech because he had created the plans for the missiles that could blanket Japan and South Korea with "Sky-fire and Destruction". It had been announced that Bora was to be given a medal, perhaps from Our Marshal himself. People were thrilled even at the possibility that they could witness such a wonderful thing.

The excitement was such that no one paid the slightest attention to the three poorly dressed Americans. Nam thought to herself that she would have had to be wearing glow-in-the-dark chartreuse to stand out enough to be noticed. They moved as quickly as they could through the crowd to get to the front of the lines without drawing undue attention to themselves. Miguel found a three-story building with a fire escape ladder that went from the ground to the flat roof and climbed it carrying his fourteen-pound box.

Nam and Pedro were finally able to insinuate themselves between two very large rural enthusiasts who had never seen a missile before and were growing ecstatic at the mere thought that they might see the Dear Respected Comrade Kim Jong Un, Chairman of the Workers' Party of Korea, Chairman of the State Affairs Commission of the Democratic People's Republic of Korea and Supreme Commander of the Korean People's Army [full, formal title] in person.

The parade was concluding as the American spies watched; goose-stepping soldiers, women in white blouses and red scarves emblematic of the important roll of women in defense of the nation, children in their pioneer uniforms who were tired but still thrilled to be there, and a coterie of tanks, missile trucks, and military jets. The parade marchers quickly dispersed and a review stand was brought onto the main thoroughfare from one of the side streets. The pulse of every North Korean became more rapid. The lesser officials began to wring their hands to work up their emotions in case it was the Chairman of the Central Military Commission; so, they would not appear to be lacking in any respect.

Several generals, the mayor, the governor, and Engineer Bora Nahn assumed their places. The Third Minister of the Interior arrived and sat in the center seat middle row. He made a series of scripted remarks about the glorious successes of the Beloved Chairman, then announced that it was time for the awarding of honors for successes related to the Musudan intermediate-range ballistic missile base, and the farm cooperative of the province.

There was great and unabashed shouting and cheering for each awardee. The exclamations of praise were particularly loud and ecstatic for Engineer Bora Nahn.

"Comrade Nahn is known throughout the engineering world as the foremost of all missile scientists and builders. Because of the unique and powerful new defensive and offensive missile systems he and his team have built, we award him the Kim Jong Il Amazing Execution Award which is given to military officers who come up with interesting and creative ways to execute evil doers such as enemies of the state and foreign adversaries. Also, as acknowledgement of his long service as a military engineer..."

The Third Minister's flow was interrupted by the appearance of a delicate young woman, or adolescent, carrying a large bouquet of fresh flowers almost as large as her. She was such a charming youth that the guards made no move to restrain her. The Third Minister beckoned to her to come to the stand to present her beautiful gift in person.

"It is for the great engineer Bora Nahn," she said in her shy girlish voice.

Nahn extended his arm to take the gift. Nam was holding a Russian 9×18mm Makarov silent pistol with integral suppressor in her right hand hidden by the flowers. The cheering continued to crescendo. Suddenly, what sounded like machine gun fire erupted from a nearby roof top; guards began to fire their automatics in the direction of the incoming fire. Nam squeezed the trigger of her Makarov and felt, rather than heard, the six bullets exit the muzzle. Bora Nahn, toppled forward clutching his chest. The dignitaries around him hit the floor. Nahn appeared to be just one more of those important persons endeavoring to protect themselves.

Nam dropped her bouquet and the pistol on the ground where she had been standing and disappeared into the screaming and weeping crowd. Somewhere in the midst of the mele, another source of machine gun fire opened up. Women screamed and fainted; men dived on their wives and children to protect them; and brutal guards kicked and punched their way towards the source of the two areas of gun fire.

The near riot remained in full force as the three assassins made their way quickly back to their truck, shedding their peasant clothes as they ran. They were on the highway headed north and well beyond Myŏngch'ŏn before the local police and military officers from the ballistic missile base could restore order.

A mere private discovered the source of the machine gun fire from the building.

"I have boxes and boxes of exploded large Chinese big sound firecrackers here."

Other soldiers found spent paper firecracker cartridges on the street below. A police lieutenant found the second source of firecracker noise in the center of the square. The investigation revealed one person trampled and sent to the hospital, one man dead—Bora Nahn—of a score of bullet injuries to the heart. The police said it was done by a Russian, but the military said that just because it was a Russian type gun did not mean that it was done by a Russian. Even DPRK criminal elements could come by such a weapon on the black market. In the end, the entire thing became a cold case. It was decided not to tell Comrade Kim about it.

Within two hours of Nam's departure for Myŏngch'ŏn, Lincoln left the impromptu camp the team built and headed southwest with Jake Tanner, Oleg Swensen, and Greg Carter. They were expecting to spend a day to a day and a half in Sunch'ŏn, a city in South Pyongan province. Sunch'on had a population of a little less than 300,000 and was home to several smokey manufacturing plants. North Korea has at least eight industrial facilities that can produce chemical agents; however, the production rate and exact types of chemical munitions remained uncertain despite considerable American and South Korean expenditure of money and men.

Sarin, tabun, phosgene, adamsite, prussic acid, and a family of mustard gases–which comprise the basis of

North Korean chemical weapons including blood and blistering agents–were produced at the Sunchon Nitroline Fertilizer Factory and the Sunchon Vinalon Plant. North Korean uranium mines—Lincoln, Jake, Oleg, and Greg's destination—were operating at full capacity. The CIA had known very well about natural uranium being processed near the cities of Sunchon and Pyongsan since the 1960's.

This CIA mission–as conjured up by the WOMs–was to assassinate the brain trust of nuclear scientists who lived there like monks or slaves. Whether or not they were willing workers was one of the questions that begged an answer. Lincoln determined to find out the state of mind of the dedicated scientists before making his final decision about killing or kidnapping them. Having seen the dangerous manufacturing plants, he began planning how to kill his main quarries, or kidnap them, and/or blow up the plants.

The three clandestine agents spent their first night in town reconnoitering both plants. Perimeter security was fairly heavy, but the guards were on a rigid time scale, which allowed the men to pass through the fence through an open hole they would have to cut. The handy CIA information they brought along with them allowed for them to know critical factors at both plants. Now that he had seen the plants, Lincoln, Jake, and Greg, found it to be of minor difficulty to penetrate the defenses. The more thorny issue was when could the spies expect their quarries to have one of their regular meetings.

Oleg was the best of the three men at linguistics and was—thankfully–one of best linguists for Korean in the unit, after Nam. He was a better reader than a speaker, which happened to suit the needs of the mission better. The trio broke into then headquarters office for three nights running and used up precious sleeping time trying to find a schedule for meetings. They discovered that the chief engineer–Lee Byung-woo–was a neat freak. He followed every suggestion ever made by Adam Smith when he was at his most anal. He had a very neat sign on his wall, in English that read:

"An instructed and intelligent people are always more decent and orderly than an ignorant and stupid one."– Adam Smith

It was evident that every night before he left work for home, he cleaned off his desk, emptied the trash, and put his office trash in the larger bin for incineration in the morning. It was there that Oleg found the agendas for the upcoming month. As a result, the three spies could encounter the plant boss and Kim Jong Ill stooge at their own convenience.

The next day, they set in motion their plan to serve the West and to throw a large stumbling block in the way of North Korean progress to advance their aggressive nuclear weapons program.

The meeting—a regular and mandatory one which was part of the plant director's schedule—was held in the Executive Administrator Mr. Park Hak-Kun's conference room on the seventh floor. For the last time, the three Americans made their weary and breathless way up the back stairway, down the hall, and into the conference room. Jake found four very inauspicious places to hide the simple C4 explosive devices, attached the remotely-detonation fuses, tapped in the simple cell-phone code; and the three men slipped away into the night to put similar explosives in every manufacturing building on the campus.

The night of the meeting, they waited until they could see the lights come on in the seventh floor office and watched through their high-power night binoculars until it was apparent that the conference room was filled with men in suits. Then, Jake made a courtesy conference call.

Lincoln, Jake, and Oleg vacated the military/industrial site before the first fire department trucks arrived. Police cars, military trucks, and three sets of hose trucks rushed into the flaming area while the three spies passed them going in the opposite direction. They were back in their camp before the sun came up.

On the same day that Lincoln, Jake, and Oleg, set off for Myŏngch'ŏn, four other spies left for Yangdŏg-ŭp in the Pothonggang District. A resourceful local CIA agent had rounded up an appropriately filthy old coal truck. The windows were so dark and dirty that no one could see in. That was useful because all the agents—John Nilsson, Henry Corbash, Dwight C. Templeton, Jr., and AJ Winthrop—were lily whites from the eastern seaboard of the United States. Winthrop even had curly red hair. Yangdŏg-ŭp was a small city with an important resource—coal—and everyone and everything in the area was dedicated to the purpose of mining, reducing the larger chunks into lumps of half an inch by half an inch, loading 100 tons into massive, long trucks, and delivering the precious coal to the Bay of Korea. The coal was especially precious to the government because it was transshipped to markets—most in the PRC—under the radar to avoid the US navy scrutiny of any product-bearing vessel trying to avoid the sanctions.

The location, its product, and its purpose, was so important to Kim Jong Un and his inner circle that Chairman Kim had assigned his nephew, General Kim Gyeong Kye, to direct operations as a task master who answered only to the Dear Leader. He was the governor of the district, mayor of the town, manager of the coal plant, and director of the trucking business. Unknown to his uncle Kim–the Superior Person–Nephew Kim had two side businesses. The first was an accounting concern whose only purpose was to skim profits off the top for lining Gen. Kim's rapidly growing bank account in Vanuatu, where banking privacy and secrecy were the paramount services of the island nation.

The second enterprise was even more lucrative. Gen. Kim and his inner circle of cronies ran a transshipment center for human trafficking. Girls and boys from China, eastern Europe, the Philippines, and South Korea—all drugged and kidnapped—were trucked and trafficked by ship to destinations in Germany, South America, Northern China, and India. Gen. Kim was scrupulous about not allowing any of his sex-slaves to be used in North Korea. The danger of exposure was too great.

The Washington WOMs had been studying Yangdŏg-ŭp and its operations for over a decade. Until this golden opportunity presented itself thanks to the new president Sybil Norcroft Daniel, no good plan had been devised. Now, a detailed game plan had been developed, and Lincoln Howard's ultra-secret organization were to be the doers.

The first task for the American spies was to reconnoiter the area. They had been provided with excellent satellite terrain photographs, compliments of Google Earth, and city/county street maps from a grocery store in the outskirts of Pyongyang. Seeing the region and the town—if it could really be so designated accurately—gave the men both optimism and serious concerns for their own developing plan.

A few strategically placed explosives would disrupt plant operations and transportation for months, if not years. The roads—which entered and exited in all four directions of the map—were wide and well maintained. It would be easy to drive off into the hinterlands and get lost in the dense forests on the mountainsides.

There was a downside, of course—a serious one. The dismal little place was crawling with young, tough, well-fed regular army soldiers who appeared to be constantly on the alert. How to get past them posed what at first seemed to be an insurmountable problem. The solution came when the unit's radioman made contact with President Daniels herself.

CHAPTER
FOUR

S ybil was fast asleep in her residence bed, spooning her handsome husband, Charles, and getting the first truly good rest for the past difficult week.

Her chief Secret Service agent tapped softly on the bedroom door. There was no response; after all, it was 0210, and he knew that the president's opinion was that there were "no one but burglars and bad women" out and about at that dreadful time of night.

He tapped again, louder. Still no response.

He gave a heavy sigh and pushed the door open.

"Madam President," he said, "you have an urgent call in the Situation Room."

There was something about the name of that room that broke through her reverie and brought her to instant full awareness,

"Yes, David, what's up?"

"Call from an agent in North Korea."

"*Lincoln*," she thought. "*Has a disaster happened, and we're exposed?*"

0200 was a time to bring to mind such negative thoughts. She did not expect an answer.

"On my way," she said.

She jumped out of bed, leaving Charles still asleep. She threw on a robe and covered her frazzled blond hair with a pashmina.

"Top of the morning, Madam President," the officers in the Situation Room chorused.

"And for the rest of the day to you, Gentlemen and Ladies, what delights do you have to share at this fine time of the morning?"

"On the sat phone, Ma'am," Lieutenant General Mark A. Dietrich, chief of the NGA [National Geospatial Intelligence Agency] said.

He handed her the receiver, and she said, "Hello, Lincoln, is that you?"

"No, Madam President, "he is elsewhere involved in the mission. I am the radioman, and I have a message from four field agents calling from Mission Station 4NK."

"Go ahead, Agent."

"We have a problem and need help, Ma'am."

"*Color me surprised,*" Sybil said to herself.

Out loud, she asked LTG Dietrich where 4NK was.

He pointed on a map and whispered, Yangdŏg-ŭp coal fields."

"Critical?" she whispered back.

"Highly."

Back into the sat phone, she said, "Tell me the problem and what is needed."

He gave a quick New York detective 'spot-and-bob' child's simplified rendition not bothering with verbs or adjectives.

"Our guys need an answer and PDQ. What to do?"

"You mean, 'what for me to do?' That about it?"

"Yes Ma'am."

"I'll get right on it and then get back to you ASAP."

"Thank you, Madam President, we knew we could count on you."

The CJCS looked her in the eyes and asked, "What is your plan, Ma'am?"

"Haven't a clue at the moment, any suggestions for a diversion, a serious one?"

"I do have an idea, but I don't think you'll like it," Gen. Gabler said.

"Of course not, what's your terrible idea?"

"Fire off a missile from one of our carriers and have it land near one of the NK's naval vessels. There are always a few on patrol outside their territorial waters. I think that would be enough to get the Great Genius Leader to mobilize the troops to save the homeland just as his near-deity Supreme Leader Kim Il Sung did to drive out the Japanese way back when."

"Think that will be enough to start WW III, General?"

"Calculated risk, but the new Greatest Leader of all Time is not stupid; crazy, maybe, but not stupid."

She sighed, "Make it happen, General, and hold on to your helmet."

"Yes, Ma'am, but I'll probably be holding on to more precious parts."

She laughed. "I always like a practical man. So, General, how long before the missile launches?"

"Just long enough to find a good near-miss target… something like an hour."

The newly appointed CNO, Christian Leavitt, transmitted the order to the *Theodore Roosevelt;* and President Daniels linked back up with the radio operator in North Korea.

"I have a plan and am executing it in one hour. You should see mobilization action by the hostiles about then because one of their ships of the line is going to come under missile fire."

"That should do it, Madam President. I'll pass the message down the line."

Agents John Nilsson, Henry Corbash, Dwight C. Templeton, Jr., and AJ Winthrop, received the president's message in Yangdŏg-ŭp half an hour later. True to her word, the sleepy world of the coal fields came alive. Squadrons of troop trucks set out for the seashore to repel American invaders. Heavy artillery and missiles appeared out of the ground and aimed skyward. The perimeter and building security guard details were cut in half to aid in the coming great struggle.

While most of the frenzy and traffic was outgoing, the American spies moved in towards the coal plants. They passed two heavily laden coal trucks ready to transport the hundreds of tons of illicit coal to the port, but which were now standing idle; their drivers and guards having fled into nearby buildings to take cover.

The spies split up and raced around apparently aimlessly like most of the workers, police, and military personnel who had been receiving conflicting orders from headquarters and from the Supreme Dear Leader himself. The spies, however, knew exactly what they were doing. They had smeared their faces with coal dust as camouflage, and each raced to a pre-determined location to plant his bomb.

The din and excitement increased around them, for the moment like a great coop full of chickens running around as if they had just had their heads cut off. The spies took full advantage of the confusion to plant enough IEDs and limpet bombs to destroy all function of the coal mines and to ignite fires in the uranium mines that struck terror into the hearts and minds of every North Korean in the vicinity.

The agents divided up and planted bombs a few inches deep in the coal on the trucks and took pains not to injure the roads headed to the shores of Korea Bay. All other roads received more than their share of explosive damage to make them incapable of repair for ten days or more.

Important nephew, General Kim Gyeong Kye, directed the chaos from the safest place he could find—the top floor of the headquarters building. He watched with pleasure as the two huge coal trucks drove away unharmed. They were followed by an old coal truck he presumed was to supply repair materials along the way. He did not give any of the trucks another thought. He and his officers and a thousand or more of his men were wrong about that optimistic thought.

The three trucks moved at full speed ahead, daring any lesser vehicle or pedestrian to get in their way. Their mission was sacred to the nation and to the Dear Leader, and nothing and no one was going to impede its progress. There was no oncoming traffic. Every vehicle of any importance was headed west to the ocean to meet the invaders before they could organize on land. Every vehicle was breaking every speed law and making seriously rapid progress.

The spies fought to keep their places immediately behind the coal carriers and were successful all the way to North Korea's second largest western sea port— Sunch'on Coal Port–located a short distance northeast of Pyongyang on the middle section of the Taedong River. The spies felt overly ambitious and wanted to be able to destroy Sunch'on *and* Nampo, the largest west coast port servicing the Pyongyang area, located on the mouth of the Taedong River considerably farther north. They were pragmatists and knew that they should feel highly successful if they could destroy just one of them, and that is what they set out to do.

After four hours of waiting their turn, the two huge trucks from Yangdŏg-ŭp pulled into the holding dock area preparatory to transfer all their coal to the immense cargo ship sitting between them. The American spies got itchy trigger fingers and yearned to make the mobile call that would cause the horrendous destruction they all wanted to witness, but they waited and went to work.

They divided up into two teams of two men each and set out to effect half of the plan set forth by the WOMs months ago. There were seven major thoroughfares and three large railways that entered and left the major hub. To be successful, the spies had to plant explosive devices soon enough, large enough, well enough hidden, and at every land route. The port was extremely busy, although there was no activity indicative of preparing to defend the port against evil American attackers. They divided up and literally ran about setting their traps and hiding them so that no one would simply stumble on to them and ruin the show.

By 1445, everything was set. John Nilsson and Henry Corbash had found a train schedule for the entire port and set timers to blow up moving loaded trains to maximize the destruction and difficulty of moving the rubble in the aftermath. Dwight C. Templeton, Jr., and AJ Winthrop chose to plant double sets of bombs about half a klick apart on every roadway and set them to trap huge trucks with their massive and valuable coal cargoes in a pincer of detonations.

John checked and rechecked the train schedules. Henry did not bother; he could hear them coming and began to count down. The men were sitting three klicks from the port—the maximum range for their disposable phones to work reliably. Dwight began to count down from thirty as the trains closed in on the port facilities.

"Five, four, three, two, one…" and every explosion occurred successfully within two seconds of every other explosion. The port disappeared in a gigantic ball of fire and caustic coal smoke and dust. Six trains loaded with prepared coal criss-crossed each other and met a cataclysmic explosion as they passed. The trains derailed, turned over, caught fire, and looked as if a naughty boy had willfully scattered his brother's favorite toy train out of spite. Truckloads of coal—perfect fuel for a long-burning, extremely hot fire—exploded shooting flames upward a thousand feet and laterally far enough to ignite surrounding buildings and spread for more than a mile circumferentially.

The investigation of the aftermath confirmed what everyone had already surmised. It was intentional, well-planned and executed, and successful beyond anything the terrorists could have hoped for. It was enough to ignite the Superior Leader's fury like almost nothing else had ever done. He was so infuriated that he demanded that the perpetrators be shot with antiaircraft artillery in a public forum and all the people forced to watch. Kim's advisors urged a great propaganda campaign against the Americans whom they were convinced were guilty.

Kim dragged his feet. He favored the hypothesis that this heinous crime was the work of internal enemies, and he was determined to torture them for weeks before the public cannonade. All outraged government officials lacked one important item; they had no evidence; and they could not link the activities to the other recent disasters. They all had their favorite targets, but real evidence was going to be hard to come by. So… they made up evidence.

Kim's political enemies—real or imagined—were rounded up and brutally questioned. Kim would not allow them to be killed. He needed a Stalin level show trial and decided to draw up confessions damning political rivals; and for the next show, his prosecutors presented several dozen confessions from well known dissidents which demonstrated a widespread conspiracy to aid the Americans in an invasion.

Kim was nothing if not a master of propaganda. He turned the entire set of disasters into heroic defenses of the nation—similar to that accomplished by his deified grandfather who drove out the Japanese. The American invasion was thwarted by Kim and his brave generals. The conspirators accused of aiding and abetting the traitors were removed from the blessings of life in the Great North Korean power-house country by the quick thinking and heroic action of the Dear Leader.

To convince his countrymen and women, who had no opportunity to see or hear contrarian information, Kim Jong Un awarded himself a second Order of the National Flag, a second the Order of Freedom and Independence 1st Class given to Division, Corps, or Army field commanders, for achievement in battle, 1st Class, an Order of Kim Il-Sung medal which was established in 1972. It was awarded for extreme heroic exploits during war became and his proudest achievement. And last, a Commemorative Order "60th Year Anniversary Of the Fatherland Liberation War Victory". No one made note of the fact that Kim was at the time thirty-seven years old.

His propaganda coup, both for his beloved followers to revel in, and to show that he could stand up the hegemonists from America without igniting a world war, he was pictured in the national media receiving the Nobel Peace Prize in Geneva. The hearers and viewers were overcome with emotion. His triumphs were duly celebrated in the DPRK's five major television stations: Korean *Central TV, Mansudae Television, Ryongnamsan TV* [Korean Educational and Cultural Network]; *Kaesong Television* [which targets South Korea, but graciously agreed to show the magnificence of the Great Leader]; and the *Sport Television* [which dedicated a full week to the extravaganza of praise for Kim.

All the national newspapers enthusiastically spread the word about their country's greatest heroes, [there are no private publications]—*Rodong Sinmun*, the organ of the Workers' Party of Korea; *Joson Inmingun*, the newspaper of the Korean People's Army; the *Chongnyon Jonwi*, the *Kimilsungist-Kimjongilist* Youth League paper; and *The Pyongyang Times* [English-language newspaper, only published in the capital].

No citizen of North Korea was traumatized by having to learn of the several criminal attacks around the country. That news was kept very general and accompanied by the party line. Such news would have included: that three large bulk cargo vessels filled to maximum capacity at the Sunch'on quay and bunkering pier disappeared in a fire ball; that outside interests reported Russian and Chinese laundering of coal shipments had abruptly halted. That was not a particularly serious set-back.

The American CIA and *Reuters International* reported that Russian coal was now being moved by ship to two ports near Vladivostok, Kholmsk, and Nakhodka, Russia. From there, the coal was successfully being transloaded onto Russian ships for sales to Japan and South Korea, and to other countries not yet fully verified. The other result of the North Korea/Russian Federation economic increase was that North Korean coal could still be mined, refined, and shipped, from Nampo, Wonsan, and Chongjin.

It appeared to most analysts, that the principle success of the attacks in North Korea– whoever the cause—was psychological and seen as bad joss. But then, psychology has driven the Hermit Kingdom since its very inception.

The CIA assassination unit finished its mission with a flurry of brilliantly planned and executed actions intended to embarrass and harass the leadership of North Korea. In that, they surely succeeded. Seven explosions and fires, 362 deaths of notable people close to Chairman Kim in addition to those ending with the Sunch'on Port mission counted as successes. President Daniels awarded all sixteen members of the unit with the Distinguished Intelligence Cross–the highest honor that can be given to an intelligence agent. But, unfortunately, all the awards had to be filed away in Ultra-Top-Secret files for a minimum of thirty years after every recipient died.

CHAPTER

FIVE

The CSA riots were still going on, but sporadically now that the trial in Atlanta was over; the verdict and the imprisonment awaiting imposition of the death penalty was yesterday's news. Even the membership of the CSA was declining—something about Americans not being particularly fond of backing a group that advocated the return of slavery. However, secession per se was definitely not off the books because of the deliberate and well researched arguments put forward in the courts by the proponents of the Cascadia bio-region.

The major newspapers and networks were now focusing on the growing national trend towards secession. A groundswell of excitement had gone so far that all fifty states were currently sending official petitions to the central government by groups with fairly large numbers of adherents desiring to leave the Union. The legality of secession had become front page news throughout the United States, and it was no longer a given that secession could not happen.

As a result of court cases adjudicated in California, the Cascadia Doug Flag–which featured an image of a Douglas Fir Tree–prominently was becoming as familiar to people who had a penchant for news or to learn things as the old Confederate rebel flag [aka, Dixie flag, and Southern Cross Flag] . The California judicial system is the largest in the US and serves a population of more than 39.5 million people— about 12 percent of the total U.S. population. The sheer size of the population involved in the suits was enough to rivet attention on the Sunshine State and the riveting issue of secession.

As with almost all judicial matters, the earliest cases related to Cascadia were heard in trial [superior] courts—58 [one for each county] in 500 court buildings. It was not surprising that the judgments resulted in a confusing range of decisions.

As a result, a select number moved on to one of the six Courts of Appeal. As in most other cases before the Courts of Appeal, the Cascadia cases involved the review of a superior court decision being contested by a party to the case.

The Superior and Appellate Court actions consumed two years of contentious, but often brilliant arguments and resulted in a deadlock—three to three—of decisions half for, and half against, allowing secession. That made a hearing before the Supreme Court of California inevitable.

When the day came, there was a circus level of activity around the State Supreme Court in the Earl Warren Building on 350 McAllister Street in San Francisco—a place hoped to be the final residence for the state's most important court, having moved twenty-two times in its 150-year history. The circus goers might well have saved their energy because her six associate justices heard arguments for five months, then deliberated for three months and came to a highly disappointing decision locked at three to three for and against secession. The Chief Justice Christine Fuller Larson broke the deadlock in favor of allowing secession which made that ruling one of the most disputed in California's history. An appeal to the United States Ninth Circuit Court was made all but mandatory. President Daniels had her solicitor general, Steven Carlisle Mathers, file an *amicus curie* brief in favor of overturning the judgment. That was the last move for the State of California. It was on to the federal courts, beginning in San Francisco, still in California.

The Ninth Circuit of Appeals–headquartered in the James R. Browning U.S. Court of Appeals Building–is by far the largest of the thirteen courts of appeals, with 29 active judgeships serving jurisdictions as far-flung as Alaska, Arizona, California, Hawaii, Nevada, Washington, Guam, and the Northern Mariana Islands, to name a few. It is felt by conservatives to favor the "loonie-toon" California progressive agenda, but its history does not support that. The issue of secession was only barely a conservative hope, but the judgment was hardly a sure thing for either side.

After reviewing the California Superior, Appellate, and Supreme court, evidence and findings and hearing forty-one days of testimony from the brightest legal scholars in the region, the Ninth Circuit Court justices deadlocked at five to five because the Chief Justice had a heart attack the day before the decision was to be rendered. Her preferences were unknown.

Throughout the United States, there was an uproar of complaints, mostly from conservatives who were opposed to the matter being heard by SCOTUS, because that could well determine the matter with finality. Much of the complaints came from opposition to the Ninth Circuit's unique rules concerning the composition of the court. It has historically been an *en banc* court [Fr, in bench, a session in which a case is heard before all the judges of a court, i.e. before the entire bench, rather than by a panel of judges selected from among them.]. Usually, in other circuits, *en banc* courts are composed of *all active circuit judges*, plus—in some jurisdictions–any senior judges who took part in the original panel decision.

In the Ninth Circuit it would be grossly impractical for twenty-nine or even or more judges to take part in any single oral argument or to deliberate on a decision *en masse*. The court decided on its on unique make-up: an *en banc* review by the Chief Judge and a panel of ten *randomly selected* judges. As a result, the Ninth Circuit's *en banc* reviews often do not actually reflect the views of the majority of the court and at times may not even include any of the three judges involved in the decision being reviewed in the first place. As a result–of Ninth Circuit Court rulings that were reviewed by SCOTUS—only twenty percent were affirmed; nineteen percent were vacated outright; and sixty-one percent were reversed. SCOTUS records revealed that the median reversal rate for all federal appellate courts was sixty-eight point 29% during the same period.

To President Sybil Daniels's dismay, there was no choice but to have the issue heard by SCOTUS on an accelerated basis. The stakes could not be higher.

The Supremes made room on their calendar for the first secession case since the civil war to be heard a fortnight later. The conservatives were not really sure that this was a conservative issue but presumed that the decision would go their way because eight of the nine justices either leaned towards or were frankly avowed conservatives following the presidency of an ardent populist. The liberals felt much the same way but were sure that their point of view would prevail because it was so much more logical. Their real problem was that they could not agree on what the liberal agenda should be.

The pithy answer of Will Rogers as to his political preferences, "I am not a member of any organized political party. I am a Democrat," seemed to be as accurate today as it was when he said it in the 1930s.

Sybil asked her solicitor general to handle the government's case for four reasons: he was the governments chief litigator; he knew the case backwards and forwards; he was a bulldog defending his bone; and he had appeared before The Court seven times. His passion was all in, and he could not even think of losing. She knew that the opposing attorney, Neal Dastrup, had all those qualities and then some.

He lived in the Cascadia area as did all his real friends and family. He lived and breathed the concept of Cascadia being a free and sovereign country. He had nearly twenty years of defending the dream in the legal battlegrounds and in the political arena. He was a top-notch lawyer who was as fully prepared and as articulate as Abraham Lincoln when he opposed secession. Sybil thought of Sherlock Holmes, "the game's afoot" and she knew this was it. She also knew it was no game.

On the day when the legal arguments began, Solicitor General Steven Carlisle Mathers, entered the Supreme Court building through the southwest door—First St., N.E.–located on the ground level, to his right as he faced the inspiring and sobering front of the building which he had done before on several occasions. He knew not to walk up the front steps and wondered if his opponent was aware of such details.

There was a fairly long line, and Mathers walked to the front of the line as if he owned the place and identified himself as arguing counsel. He then reported to the Lawyers' Lounge on the first floor Courtroom level at the appointed hour, 0905. He and the clerk waited for Mr. Dastrup until 0917 which earned the man a stern frown. The Clerk briefed the two counsels and led them back to the Lawyers' Lounge where they were to wait until summoned. Both men made concerted efforts not to appear anxious or nervous, but neither thought his air of nonchalance would survive chitchat with his opponent.

The two arguing counsels were settled in the Courtroom and seated in their assigned seats at the counsel tables about ten minutes before Court is scheduled to convene. The Marshal of the Court cried the Court at 10 a.m. The

Chief Justice made his routine announcements. Opinions of the two opposing sides were then released. Authoring Justice Danecraft read a summary of the opinions taking five minutes for each opinion. Motions for admission to the Bar were heard and the two counselors were officially read in. The Chief Justice announced that the Court will hear argument in the first case for argument that day.

Mather was on tap first.

Chief Justice Fens-Griffith announced, "Solicitor General of the United States, Steven Carlisle Mathers."

Mathers took two deep breaths, coughed into his elbow, and rose from his seat facing the nine justices. The Solicitor General looked Chief Justice Alexander Wolton Fens-Griffith directly in the eyes, stood at the lectern without being invited, and began to speak:

"Mr. Chief Justice, may it please the court," he said as did almost every petitioner before the court, "I represent the United States and intend to present convincing arguments as to why this court should not allow any state or any portion of the United States as presently constituted by law to secede. We have been through this before and the Union vowed that it would never happen again."

"Mr. Mather, do you mean to tell us that you are wiser than the judges of the Ninth Circuit court who deadlocked on this very complicated issue."

"No, Justice Holmby; but my argument is correct enough under the Constitution that this Court should have no difficulty in finding for the government, for the Constitution, and for the laws and traditions that have upheld every attack on the cohesion of the national government even at the risk of civil war. I hardly need to point out that the Union won that war and returned the nation to its rightful cohesive state."

"Do I take it that you are in agreement with the ruling in Texas v. White?" asked Sandra Knight, the longest sitting justice on the Court.

"I do, and I think it asserts a precedent that the Court should uphold."

"Explain to the Court why Texas v. White should be precedent for us today 114 years later."

"Thank you, Madam Justice for the opportunity to make clear this pivotal ruling. The one and only time since the Court's first docketed case in 1791 was when the legality of secession was challenged before the Supreme Court occurred in December 1868, Texas v. White. Simply put, the reconstruction government in Texas claimed that bonds owned by Texas since 1850—prior to the secession by Southern states–had been illegally sold by the Confederate State Legislature there during the illegal war, the matter regarding the legality of Texas's secession became the deciding factor.

"The defeated confederates who sought to keep those bonds failed to meet the test of the Court. The majority opinion—written by Supreme Court Chief Justice Salmon P. Chase–struck down the Texas Ordinance of Secession, calling it 'null,' and crafted a decision that rendered *all acts of secession illegal* according to the 'perpetual union' of both the Articles of Confederation and subsequent Constitution for the United States. I argue that there has never been a cogent argument to countermand that order by the then sitting Supreme Court of the United States."

"As a matter of law, Counselor, do you think this Court should uphold the concept of perpetuity, the word used in the very name of the Articles of Confederation?"

"I do, and I applaud the language of the Preamble to the Constitution of the United States, and I quote, 'We the People of the United States, in Order to form a more perfect Union...' That is the clearest evidence possible placed as the first sentence of the Preamble and of the body of the Constitution itself, that the Constitution—as the basis for all United States law–enjoins us as the basis for all United States law, enjoins us to form a perfect union."

"This is the place for nit-picking, Counselor. The exact language is 'a more perfect union'. Could that wording not open the way for secession by the argument that a secession would make our union a more nearly perfect union?" Justice Scarborough asked pointedly.

"No, Sir, Justice Scarborough, the passage of time has upheld the concept that 'more perfect' refers to the less perfect period under the Articles of Confederation and Perpetuity and that the Constitution was mankind's greatest effort to preserve the best and most important democracy and federal republic. Cohesion of the union is part and parcel of that lofty goal."

For nearly two hours the learned solicitor general fielded questions from the justices without referring to notes, and without making mistakes as he quoted the Constitution and other relevant precedent case law.

Chief Justice Alexander Wolton Fens-Griffith asked the last questions: "Do you have anything to add, Mr. Solicitor General?"

"No, your honor."

The Chief turned to his fellow justices, "Any further questions for the government?"

Eight justices answered "no".

"Then, it is time to adjourn for lunch. Mr. Dastrup, are you prepared to appear at one o'clock sharp to make your case?"

"Yes, Sir, Mr. Chief Justice."

CHAPTER
SIX

At one o'clock on the dot, Chief Justice Fens-Griffith announced: "Mr. Neal Dastrup, Counsel for the petitioner."

Mr. Dastrup immediately stood up and walked to the lectern and began to speak, "Mr. Chief Judge," then turned scarlet. "I beg your pardon, I'm a little nervous. Mr. Chief Justice,"... there was a brief and unhelpful pause, "May, may it please the Court."

There was a slightly audible sigh of relief from the spectators.

"I am Neal Dastrup speaking for the citizens of the proposed new sovereign nation of Cascadia," another *faux pas*; attorneys are not supposed to give their names or anything about themselves.

Dastrup knew he had to get control of himself, or his petition would fail due to his inability to get his message before the Court in a convincing manner.

"The people of the region in the United States we call Cascadia seek relief from the Court to be permitted to separate from the United States of America, to form a new sovereign nation recognized by the United States as such, and to be permitted to go their own way."

Things were going more smoothly. Dastrup was finding his rhythm.

"We desire to convince the Court that it is Constitutional—in the strictest sense—for Cascadia to secede from the United States. The United States of America is governed as federal republic, and therefore some even argue that the U.S. is not a democracy. A republic is defined as a political system in which the supreme power is vested upon the *citizenry* that is entitled to vote for its representatives and officers responsible to them, while a democracy is defined as a government of the people and by the people exercised through elected or direct representatives. In short, it is the people who may make the choice to secede or not. And that is Constitutional.

"How is it that the people of the area we call Cascadia see secession as Constitutional and not a threat to the United States and certainly neither treason nor anything else than our legal righ? Cascadia a bio-region which includes the present states of Washington, Oregon, Northern California, parts of Idaho and Montana, Southern Alaska, and also includes British Columbia and parts of Alberta, Canada. There are natural characteristics as well as the legal ones which make secession and forming a new nation logical, practical, and legal.

"The bioregion is created naturally within the watersheds of the Columbia and Fraser river valleys that flow through British Columbia, Washington, and Oregon. Its boundaries stretch from South East Alaska in the North, to Northern California in the South, and east as far as the Yellowstone Caldera. This fact gives the Cascadia bio-region natural continental and tectonic boundaries.

"Another viable argument for our movement towards secession is that Cascadia will soon become one of the world's largest economies, generating nearly $1 trillion dollars in GDP. The sovereign area can take care of its own needs, conduct its own commerce, and supply its own defense, so long as ours is a defensive, not an offensive system as the United States has become. We intend a laisse fair attitude and to remain neutral. The United States–which we must leave–insists on being the world's policeman.

"Cascadia's primary industries—and already successful–will continue to be farming and technology. The government will focus on environmentalism to save it from the descent into destruction of the planet going on in the US and most of the rest of the world."

"Counselor, this sounds like something of a utopian pipe dream. Could it be that you are about to lead the citizens of that vast area over a cliff like lemmings?" Justice Sykes asked.

"On the contrary, Justice Sykes–as I said a moment ago–we eschew the massive national defense system of the US, and the unconscionable accumulation of debt that entails. Another viable argument for our movement towards secession is that Cascadia will soon become one of the world's largest economies, generating nearly $1 trillion dollars in GDP. We have established a preparatory Ministry of Finance which is already in charge of the economy and money in Cascadia. As in other developed countries, some of the most common of the of the Ministry's duties include setting up the establishment of taxation and collecting the income, welfare services—which we expect to be limited owing to the rather homogeneous excellent work ethic among Cascadia people, and social security services, printing and production of banknotes and maybe coins; the United States spends a ridiculous amount of money making coins–using more money to produce them than their face worth–and management of precious metal and other natural resources."

"Counsel," asked Justice Brown, "I can't believe I am even asking this, but what kind of economic research have you done that would make you think your new country would work? We all remember the last time the Quebecoise attempted to secede from Canada; the venture failed at the polls because calmer heads–even of the Quebecoise–saw the folly looming: inability to raise money, almost no capacity for national defense; and the ardent proponents had not even figured in the cost of security and welfare."

"Our facts speak for themselves, Justice Brown, The entire region maintains an unemployment rate of 3.4%, an Ease of Doing Business Rank of 4th in the world, estimated exports of $188 billion f.o.b. [free on board—meaning that the buyer is at risk and takes ownership of the goods once they goods are shipped], imports of $169 billion f.o.b., and economic aid of $1.6 billion ODA [Official Development Assistance]."

"You have done your homework with regards the proposed Cascadia, Counselor, but we have barely touched the question we came to discuss today, viz. is your secession or any secession legal and constitutional? This is the time to make your argument, Sir," Justice Brown asked pointedly indicating that neither he nor the Court was going to be taken in by obfuscation.

"Thank you, Justice Brown. I will now proceed with the arguments that should convince the Court to recognize our petition. If the Court will permit, I would like to begin with a telling question: Why wasn't Jefferson Davis, the President of the Confederacy convicted of treason for his part in the secession?"

Justice Lathrope took the bait, "The simplest answer was that he was never tried, hence never convicted."

"We could belabor this for most of the day, Justice Lathrope, but the Occam's razor of it is that the federal government feared he could convince a jury that secession was *not* illegal. This problem has been hiding in shadows for a long time, and no definitive Supreme Court decision has ever been made. I would argue that now is the time for it."

"Texas v. White made a clear-cut decision, Counselor," Lathrope rebutted.

"True, but not necessarily pertinent, Justice. There were flaws."

"Really. That is difficult from me to believe given that it has served as precedent for well over a hundred years without effective challenge."

"With respect to the justice and to the Court, I must say, 'until today'. In fact, a great many Americans–including jurists–do not think that Texas v. White completely—or fairly—resolved the issue. We would not be here today if it had done so. Nor would California, Alaska, and most of the states in the union be moving cases towards the Court if the matter had been decided in 'perpetuity' as has been argued by a sitting justice of this Court. The issue remains that many states have serious disagreements about federal governance as opposed to state's rights and responsibilities. I submit that the question has relevance today.

"That December in 1868, the Texas court struck down and vacated 'The Texas Ordinance of Secession', calling it 'null,' and crafted a decision that rendered all acts of secession illegal. Allow me to point out that the basis of that ruling was by making reference to the use of the term 'perpetual union' in both the Articles of Confederation and later in the Constitution of the United States. What has usually been left out, Justice Lathrope, is that Justice Chase left a small but important opening.

"In his majority opinion, he indicated an exception to the otherwise overriding finality of the rest of the opinion, 'revolution or the consent of the States'. I do not disagree that without either of those situations, secession could never be considered a legal act. Despite court rulings citing Texas v. White, it should not be accepted without scrutiny that courts are always right, or that Texas v. White is the be-all and end-all of thought on the matter.

I submit that courts are not always right. Take the Dred Scot Decision as a flagrant example. A more recent court properly revisited that heinous miscarriage of justice and corrected the error. Sometimes they are frankly inventive: take the Roe v. Wade decision. The Warren Court invented a right not contained in the Constitution of the right to privacy. The argument by the majority at that time was that the Constitution is a living and progressing thing. Really?, or is it to be taken as it is written? Of course other decisions have been overturned. It is part of the work of the Court to keep the law alive, just, and constitutional.

"The Supreme Court opinion relied on the supposed *perpetual nature of the union.* As I indicated the formal name of this document cited is 'The Articles of Confederation and Perpetual Union.' The founding fathers saw fit to include what amounts to a clarification in the Preamble to the Constitution by saying the Constitution was an *attempt* to 'form a more perfect union'.

"Two questions arise that are highly pertinent to what is being argued today. First, 'why must a perpetual union be inherently the most perfect kind of union?' Second and more to our point, the union under the Articles of Confederation was not perpetual at all. The 'perpetual Union' of the confederation survived for less than a decade, which required the language in the Preamble, 'to create a *more perfect* union' than the confederation. If that is so, what is different about our petition to develop a more perfect union by seceding."

"I admit that you have proffered a true head scratcher, Counselor; but it will take more than that to convince me to vote in favor of secession, Sir. Feel free to continue to educate the Court," Justice Lathrope said with a note of growing doubt, or maybe a concern about a sacred cow in his own thinking.

"Thank you, Justice. I will get into the fine but clear points. I say that the constitutionality of secession should be broken down into three main legal arguments. Minds greater than mine have concluded that if any one of the three arguments proves to be valid, then secession is legal. The first argument calls into question the very nature of the constitution. The second argument is related to the first and has to do with the sovereignty of individuals and states, in relationship to states and the federal government respectively. The final argument has to do with what the constitution says–or rather does not say–about secession."

"Tell me honestly, Counselor, are these arguments more than just sophistry?" Chief Justice Fens-Griffith asked with more than a little acerbity.

"Oh, yes, Chief Justice Fens-Griffith. These questions go to the core of the matter. First, as to the nature of the Constitution, allow me to remind the Court that there is a substantial difference between a *compact* and a *contract*. A *compact* is an agreement between two or more entities, which is *voluntarily* maintained—I emphasize the word 'voluntarily'. On the other hand, a contract is an agreement, between two or more entities, which is *legally binding*. Aside from annoying social criticism, there is very little in the way of repercussion to breaking a compact. However, I hardly need to point out that there are serious legal repercussions to violating a contract.

"By the intentional construction of the United States Constitution, the document is a compact, not a contract.

In the Constitution there exists no legal framework in place, and external to the contract, hence there is nothing to enforce it. The constitution defines the *validity of law*, within the "many states." Therefore, it must be a compact, and as such as voluntarily maintained.

The Constitution makes no *post hoc ergo propter hoc* statement. [The Latin term *post hoc ergo propter hoc* translates to 'after this, *therefore* because of this,' which would be a logical fallacy.] The framers took care to avoid such a mistake. This supposition of cause mistakenly assumes that a thing was caused by something else that occurred before, like for instance Texas v. White as a precedent.

"The argument used by the confederacy was that the constitution was a compact between the many states, and therefore a state or all the states could decide to leave. There is no extra-constitutional law which can enforce the Constitution, and therefore the Constitution cannot be a contract. It must be a compact.

"The Constitution establishes a federal government, which acts as their supreme agent. But the states are agents of the *people* as well, and it is through the decisions of the states that the Constitution was established. Note that the people were the agents of construction of the Constitution. When a state chooses to leave the union, it does not do so on its own authority. It does so on the authority of its principals: the *citizens* of that state. And therefore–regardless of the fact that the members of the state did not directly choose to secede–the secession is still an action agreed upon by the people, as any action taken by an agent would be."

The Chief Justice asked a technical question about the Constitution, "Counsel, it has been argued since the concept of secession began to loom before the civil war that the thirteen original states were being referred to as 'existing states' and that no state could ever leave the union because of the privilege granted new states by the original thirteen. How do you answer that challenging argument to your desire to have Cascadia secede, Sir?"

"Chief Justice Fens-Griffith, the argument that a state carved from the common property of the United States does not have the same sovereignty as the original thirteen states is specious. Our third president, Thomas Jefferson–while serving at the bidding of Congress as the as Minister Plenipotentiary for Negotiating Treaties of Amity and Commerce–made clear in his Northwest Ordinance of 1787 that new states would enter the Union on 'equal footing' with all other existing states. That is to say that they had the same rights, privileges, and immunities, as the original thirteen. That included the rights of interposition and withdrawal."

"Counsel, I take exception with the argument that states have the right of interposition which, if accepted, would be a strong argument for your petition. For the record, interposition is a *claimed* right of a state of the United States to oppose actions of the federal government that the state deems unconstitutional. Under the theory of interposition, a state assumes the right to 'interpose' itself between the federal government and the people of the state by taking action to prevent the federal government from enforcing laws that the state considers unconstitutional.

In *Cooper v. Aaron*, 358 U.S. 1 (1958), the Supreme Court of the United States rejected interposition explicitly. The Supreme Court and the lower federal courts have consistently held that the power to declare federal laws unconstitutional lies with solely with the federal judiciary, not with the states. The courts have held that interposition is not a valid constitutional doctrine when invoked to block enforcement of federal law. Interposition is closely related to the theory of nullification, which holds that the states have the right to nullify federal laws that are deemed unconstitutional and to prevent enforcement of such laws within their borders."

"Justice Barnswell, I agree when the entity claiming to interpose or to nullify is a state; but the language of the Constitution is insufficiently clear to exclude 'the people' from demanding relief from an improper law by interposition or nullification. Viewed in that way, there remains a method of relief for the people; and that strengthens my argument.

"With due deference to Supreme Court Justice Antonin Scalia, he wrote a letter in 2006 arguing that the question of secession was not even in the realm of legal possibility because: First, the United States would not be party to a lawsuit on the issue; Second, the 'constitutional' basis of secession had been 'resolved by the Civil War'; and third, there is no right to secede, as 'the Pledge of Allegiance clearly illustrates through the line, one nation, indivisible'. No offense intended, but that is a popular, and emotional argument–not a legal one–and therefore must be taken as specious."

"Justice Scalia's 2006 letter was an opinion, not a judgment by the Supreme Court, Counselor," the Chief Justice reminded Mr. Dastrup. "the concept of 'one people' underlying the indissoluble union was best articulated by Supreme Court Justice Joseph Story in his famous Commentaries on the Constitution of the United States. Story–like both Chief Justice John Marshall and Alexander Hamilton before him–reasoned that the Constitution was framed and *ratified by the people at large*, not the people of an individual state and thus held the same legal position of a state formed from many counties. He said, 'The constitution of a confederated republic, that is, of a national republic, formed of several states, is, or at least may be, not less an irrevocable form of government, than the constitution of a state formed and ratified by the aggregate of the several counties of the state.'"

"Yes, Sir, Mr. Chief Justice, in that one sentence, Story reduced the states to the status of a county, shire, or province, and diminished the standing of 'the people' in one fell swoop. That general argument was used as a hammer both during Reconstruction and after against the sovereignty of the states and ignored 'the people' per se as of negligible standing. It is my contention that ignoring 'the people' in that way was an incorrect assumption of the purpose of the Constitution and of its intentions."

Chief Justice Alexander Wolton Fens-Griffith, countered, "Chief Justice Chief Justice Story agreed with Salmon Chase in 1869 that the term 'perpetual' found in the *Articles of Confederation*, deemed the Union to be indissoluble. Justice Story defended his position with the 'Supremacy Clause' found in *Article VI*, which states that all laws or treaties made 'in pursuance of the Constitution' were the 'supreme law of the land,' and he pointed to the letter sent by the Philadelphia Convention accompanying the Constitution to the state ratifying conventions that the Constitution aimed at a "consolidation of the Union." Hence, to Story and Chase, the Union continued to exist in an altered—i.e. consolidated—form and could not be dissolved.

"Another argument against secession centers on the language of *Article I, Section 10*, which clearly declares that 'No state shall enter into any treaty, alliance, or confederation...' To proponents of this position, *Article I, Section 10* unequivocally shows that the states which formed the Confederate States of America were in clear violation of the Constitution, thus invalidating their government and the individual acts of secession which led to it. Abraham Lincoln indirectly defended this position by declaring the seceding states were in 'rebellion' and therefore still members of the Union. The Constitution, then, was still legally enforceable in those states, including *Article I, Section 10*."

"I agree with that argument, except to point out that the entire section of the Constitution was dealing with the 'states', not 'the people', Mr. Chief Justice. And, let me add, Sir, one could quite easily concede that the original thirteen states may have an argument for secession due to the *Declaration of Independence* and Thomas Jefferson's language establishing thirteen 'free and independent states'. That, of course, was inherently unfair, because the 'states' were all equal. If 13 could secede, why not any or all do so? Secession–as accomplished by the Southern states in 1860 and 1861 and as discussed by the North at the Hartford Convention in 1815–is an independent act by the people of the states.

As for those who suggest that a state carved from the common property of the United States does not have the same sovereignty as the original thirteen states, Thomas Jefferson made clear in his Northwest Ordinance of 1787 that new states would enter the Union on "equal footing" with the existing states, meaning that they had the same rights, privileges, and immunities, as the original thirteen, including the right of interposition and withdrawal."

Justice Miriam Liebowitz, the only woman, the only Jew, and the only justice on the United States Supreme Court to have a PhD in law, joined the conversation. "The United States would never be a party to a lawsuit on the issue because secession, both de facto and de jure, is an extra-legal act of self-determination, and once the States have seceded from the Union, the Constitution is no longer in force in regard to the seceded political body. This same rule applies to the *Article I, Section 10* argument against secession. If the Constitution is no longer in force—the States have separated and resumed their independent status—then the Supreme Court would not have jurisdiction and therefore could not determine the 'legality' of the move. The Union, then, through a declaration of war could attempt to force the seceded States to remain, but even if victorious that would not solve a philosophical issue. The very purpose of this Court on this Day is to prevent any progress by any entity towards secession. Our president has stated with finality that she will not allow it during her administration, and I–for one— intend to aid her towards that end. It is a sacred duty."

Counsel Dastrup could not allow that to pass without comment, "War and violence do not and cannot crush the natural right of self-determination. There is nothing more American or more constitutional than that. Violence can confuse the definitions of the law and of society. It can force the vanquished into submission so long as the boot is firmly planted on their collective throats—remember the Soviets, the Nazis, and the fascists; but a bloody nose and a prostrate people settles nothing.

"Oliver Ellsworth of Connecticut said in 1788 that he feared a 'coercion of arms' in relation to a delinquent state. 'This Constitution does not attempt to coerce sovereign bodies, states, in their political capacity. No coercion is applicable to such bodies, but that of an armed force. If we should attempt to execute the laws of the Union by sending an armed force against a delinquent state, it would involve the good and the bad, the innocent and the guilty, in the same calamity.' Ellsworth recognized, as did the majority of the founding generation, that force did not destroy sovereignty. It created artificial supremacy, but sovereignty remains the underlying rule. I submit to you that sovereignty and freedom of united individuals trumps all other issues in the end, even force."

Justice Liebowitz said emphatically, "James Madison argued that the Union of the United States was a different—a new–type of contract. He said, 'We are not to consider the Federal Union as analogous to the social compact of individuals: for if it were so, a majority would have a right to bind the rest, and even to form a new constitution for the whole... The Constitution was framed by the unanimous consent of the States present in convention assembled in Philadelphia, but it had no teeth until the States, in convention, ratified it.'"

Justice Liebowitz was not about to concede anything about secession, "Another telling argument against secession comes from the language of *Article I, Section 10* where it says, 'No *state* shall enter into any treaty, alliance, or confederation....' In that segment of the Constitution is clear that the states which formed the Confederate States of America were in clear violation of the Constitution, thus invalidating their government and the individual acts of secession which led to it. That seems to me to be definitive."

Counselor Dastrup was ready for that argument, "Opponents of that interpretation such as my and the penitents I represent argue that it is the *people* who live in the states—such as California and the other states and portions of countries—not the states themselves, who have the right to secede. For to lose that right would be to lose one's sovereignty. Aside from the fact that such a loss would violate the constitutional rights of that individual, it would be tantamount to becoming a slave. We Americans could only lose our sovereignty under extreme duress, that is as a result of overwhelming force, and only once we give up and submit to illegal force.

"With that exception noted—at all other times—we defer by our choice to others, who act on our behalf. For

American citizens, those agents are the several states. The states have also deferred their ultimate decision-making process to another agent–the federal government. There is nothing in the Constitution that can prevent individuals from exercising their choice to take back their decision-making authority. When a state decides to leave the union, it can do so, as long as its principals, allows it to—and only then. I submit to the honorable court that the federal government has no authority under constitutional law to stop it. That is because the federal government is merely the agent of that state, which in turn is the agent of the people—the ultimate free agents."

Chief Justice Fens-Griffith noted a pause in the questioning and asked his usual last two questions, "Do the justices have more questions?"

There were nine "nos".

"Does the counsel for the petitioners have further argument?"

Dastrup said, "No, Chief Justice. Thank you and the Court for your kind attention."

"Then the Court is adjourned. We will deliver our decision in three months."

Three months later when Sybil learned of the decision by SCOTUS in favor of the petitioner, Cascadia; she went into a deep blue funk. The majority decision—6 to 3—written by Chief Justice Fens-Griffith was in favor of secession for Cascadia. The details of the process were not spelled out, but would be the subject of a legal brief from SCOTUS before the end of the year.

CHAPTER
SEVEN

The month of July brought President Daniels two headaches: the SCOTUS decision against everything Abraham Lincoln and she had treasured as being the very definition of American government, and the realization that she was going to have to engage fully in her last knock-down-drag-out presidential campaign if she was going to get her goals accomplished.

There was considerable bitterness being expressed in the right-wing, moderate-center, and left-wing press, about her having lost a large portion of the land area of the United States, the first president ever to do so. Never mind that the secession was not yet a fait accompli. The people of the states involved—California, Oregon, and Washington, Idaho, Montana, Wyoming—and British Columbia, and Alberta, Canada had to agree on the creation of a new nation; and all parties had to determine just how that would be done and when. However, the Cascadia Doug Fir flag began to fly at sporting events, political rallies, and for holiday parades. SCOTUS predicted ten years in the making. That was ignored generally because it was too complex for ordinary readers– especially strongly ideological ones–to grasp and dissect.

Spokespersons for Cascadia started on the stump less than an hour after SCOTUS made its announcement that there would be a sea-change in the shape and function of the United States. President Daniels was given no credit by the victorious Cascadians and full blame by the rest of the potential voters. The ever eager and dogged press dug back into the past to find areas to blame her for the ongoing tensions between the US, North Korea, and Iran, with their potential for large military involvement. Her real enemies resurrected the *National Enquirer Magazine's* salacious photos and narratives with no regard for the fact that the magazine itself had repudiated the entirety of the content it had printed.

And another muckraker yellow journal tabloid dug into the past and found twenty-five-year-old headline stories accusing Sybil Norcroft BS, MD, FACS, FAANS, and avid feminist, of murdering a well-known medical malpractice attorney. The article reveled in the ghastly details of the murder: in the words of the homicide detective, "Shotgun to the back of the head. Not much left front or back. Wife identified him from a couple of tattoos and a set of very expensive teeth. Looks like forced entry through a back-bathroom window and a robbery gone bad. A secret safe had been opened, maybe under duress; and the wife says that something on the order of two mil in cash, watches, and diamonds is missing."

Detectives uncovered the semi-sordid details of the attorney's unrelenting pursuit of the famous doctor with multiple rather silly malpractice suits bent on destroying her; mostly based on the apparent motive, they presented the evidence to an ambitious prosecutor who indicted her. Sybil had endured a perp walk, lurid headlines, and a trial, in which the jury retired to deliver a verdict.

After ten days, the *National Enquirer* remained silent. After the initial flurry of news with questionable fact bases, the *New York Times, Los Angeles Times, Chicago Herald,* and *Washington Post* began serious fact checking before printing another word about President Daniels.

The right-wing publications intensified their attacks: the *Chicago Tribune,* the *New York Post,* the *Las Vegas Review-Journal,* the *Dallas Morning News,* the *National Review,* The *American Spectator,* The *American Conservative,* The *New American, and Newsmax,* kept up and increased their attacks competing for the most lurid opinions and descriptions. It was a time of carte blanche without having to even pretend to be objective for Glen Beck's *The Blaze, Fox News, Breitbart News Network, Western Journal Conservative Tribune,* and the *Drudge Report.* They went wild.

The notable left-wing publications were ambivalent; President Daniels and SCOTUS seemed to favor their general ideological opinions about secession, even though they had not bothered to research even her public pronouncements against any dissolution of the union. They decided to print only the well-researched facts on the president and about the implications of the SCOTUS decision. As a consequence, their focus turned more to economic problems, the progress of national reconstruction and repair of infrastructure, foreign policy, and tried to help their readers understand what was going on in North Korea and Iran.

At the end of the month, SCOTUS published its intended court agenda for the first Monday in October. Sybil was dismayed but hardly surprised to learn that the justices would hear four more secession cases early in the month. They were:

The AIP [Alaska Independence Party]: which argues that the original incorporation of the state was illegal, and—more importantly–that the federal government has forgotten about the Constitution of the US. The AIP proposes that the entire state of Alaska become a completely independent nation. That would make it the sixth largest country in the world based on land mass. The economy of the new nation of Alaska will be primarily related to energy resources. Fishing, agriculture, and tourism are already vital parts of their economy and are expected to increase in financial value and in the provision of jobs and is—in the minds and rhetoric of the AIP—assured of economic prosperity and stability.

The government of the new Republic of Alaska will be firmly a constitutional government supporting conservative, libertarian, gun ownership, and Christian ideals. Support for this movement is relatively large and strong and appears to be growing in comparison to most other movements, numbering well over 13,000 committed adherents. They will use the current state flag as their national banner.

The Kingdom of Hawaii: The supporters of separation are applying to the Court on the basis that there has been an active Hawaiian Sovereignty Movement for many years and that the kingdom regularly hosts constitutional conventions to return to the historical monarchy which existed until the islands were annexed by the United States. It is their contention that the annexation was illegal and was wrested by force from the Hawaiian people. The supporters have simple but ardently desired goals: restore original Hawaiian traditions, provide free health care for all, and a number of other rather generous social democratic benefits. The proposal plans for inclusion of all the eight major islands and all territory within the state.

Its economy will be based on tourism and agriculture. The people proposing the Kingdom point out that the State of Hawaii generates around $70 billion in GDP. They have full confidence that they can function in perpetuity with the parliamentary monarchy restored. Their flag is the Hawaiian flag hung upside down.

The State of Jefferson movement: has been a long simmering effort for secession. In 1941, the idea of forming a new and different US state including southern Oregon and northern California was put forward. The pertinent counties were in agreement, and the movement might well have succeeded except for the bombing of Pearl Harbor and the inevitable World War II.

The idea never died out despite the massive historical impediment. SCOTUS is being petitioned to make the

State of Jefferson into a completely logical addition of a 51st state. The argument by the counties of northern third of California north is that their one-third of the presently functioning state is undergoing taxation without representation. Declarations must be filed under Article One, Section Three of the California Constitution for a redress of grievances due to lack of representation, and the State of Jefferson has submitted the required declarations to the state supreme court which are well underway. SCOTUS fully aware that the Jefferson State is on its way.

Freedom Texas: is the most recent and currently the most active of the US secession movements. Its goal is to separate Texas from the Union. It has significant grassroots support and numbers of volunteers. They have been working with veterans' organizations and small community groups throughout the state to begin the long process of public education about their idea of "true secession".

Around the State of Texas, there was a very strong and popular conservative ideological preference. For decades, Texas citizens had demonstrated lack of faith in the federal government, more recently disagreement with the Affordable Care Act reigniting the flames of desire for secession, and even more recently and much more intensely, the upholding of same-sex marriage by the Supreme Court of the US.

The vast majority of Texans—and probably all conservatives—are, at heart, flag waving patriots who had become so disenchanted with the overreaches of the federal government that they were coming to agree with the conservative majority to break away from the rest of the union. The directors of the movement reported that almost all Texas political groups agreed that an independent Texas nation was a viable goal and a real probability, no longer just a dream.

They launched a successful state referendum [since Texas does not have an initiative process]. The outcome of the referendum obligated the current elected Texas officials to notify Congress of *people* of Texas's intent to withdraw from the union. Congress denied the initiative—according to the Freedom Texas Movement—and a lawsuit began locally and was moving by leaps and bounds to end up finally in the Supreme Court for the first Monday in October.

SCOTUS now had to make a decision on an economic pathway to secession. This second pathway is based on an all but unique governmental tax law: The State of Texas has no income tax. Unlike Freedom Texas, the federal government runs a massive deficit hence there was no reason for invasion from the US IRS. The new nation of Freedom Texas had plans in place to implement a tariff policy. The current economy of Texas is two trillion dollars. Freedom Texas insisted that the Texas GDP would rise by eradicating the kinds of waste which the federal government generates every year with no end in sight. The Freedom Texas aficionados asserted that their strong economy would be able to raise enough money to cover social security payments, military retirements, Medicare, and all direct federal programs that are contractually obligated to be paid to the people. Eliminating waste, overuse, abuse, fraud, foreign aid, welfare offenses—paying people not to work—and trying to be the world's policeman would further enhance the new republic's GDP.

The nationalist/republic movement has significantly over 300,000 supporters who have had the greatest successes in the cultural, economic, and political spheres throughout their state. They believe that secession is on the near horizon since SCOTUS has declared its intention to evaluate the claims of Freedom Texas.

The voters of the United States, looking to the polls in the coming November, were divided 70% opposed, and 30% favoring the new proposed secessions coming before the Court. President Daniels could only join the majority and to make a "No Secession" plank at the top of her platform issues. She could not really continue the position of being an unaffiliated/independent candidate. It became imperative that she register as a Democrat to garner votes from the Democrats and undecided who did not like the abrasive authoritative stance taken by the pro-secessionists. And, besides, those voters remained opposed to secession of any part of the United States in favor of what—it seemed to them—to be blatant racist, and pipedream, fantasies. For the first time, Sybil became an active politician and to begin flying all around the country and its territories to bring out the anti-secessionist voters and to convince the undecided that it was in their best interests to save the union.

Every week, Sybil watched the news political polls shift in favor of the secessionists. What charisma and public approval she had ever enjoyed was beginning to evaporate. Her republican opponent hammered home every day that keeping Sybil Daniels as the incumbent president would be a vote against the true character of the United States. Sybil was concerned that she would fail to be re-elected, but more so because it seemed likely that she would govern over the last intact United States. By mid-August, her approval rating had dropped to 30% in fairly a direct parallel with the now declining popularity of the anti-secessionist minority.

She was getting depressed enough to begin trying to figure out what she could do if she were to lose the election. Her husband, Charles, and her daughter, Cerisse, and her husband, were becoming concerned enough to begin hinting that she either drop out of the race, or begin therapy, or both.

In the first week of October, SCOTUS decided in favor of three of the four secessionist movements—Alaska Independence, Texas Freedom Movement, and Kingdom of Hawaii secessionists, primarily based on the precedent set by the Cascadia decision. The State of Jefferson proposal was not approved, but the case was sent back to the lower court to evaluate further its viability for independence while holding open the potential of being heard again by SCOTUS the following year.

Sybil said to Charles, "My dear man, I feel lower than a snake's belly in a wagon rut. My most important issues are crumbling, and soon I will have no legacy to leave."

He replied, "Sybil—my favorite president—maybe you should consider therapy. You strike me as having descended into real clinical depression."

She said, "I'll consider it if nothing happens to alter the apparent course of the campaign. Sound okay to you?"

"Even wise," said her ever supportive husband.

However–in early October–four things happened to tilt the balance: First, out of nowhere, a well-financed movement sprang up from the political center movers and shakers in the nation. They were increased in numbers by inclusion of university professors, successful CEOs, long term government elites—especially from the ranks of the State Department–career diplomats, senior military officers, importers and exporters, and well-educated members of the heretofore silent majority. The concept was simple enough when described superficially: Create a new mega-nation from a cohesive union—as opposed to a loose confederation—of Canada, the United States of America, and the United States of Mexico.

Second, Kim Jong Il's hold on his military appeared to be slipping as demonstrated by a Stalinist-like purge of more that sixty percent of his top generals and colonels in the KPA [Korean People's Army] particularly from among the Korean People's Strategic Rocket Forces–a major division of the KPA that controls the DPRK's nuclear and conventional strategic missiles—and from among the highest officials of the Ministry of Foreign Affairs, according to *Al Jazeera*.

Third, Kim Jong Il formally announced to the world via his Central Broadcasting Committee of Korea that the DPRK had successfully developed and tested a nuclear warhead and had missile capacity to put ICBMs into the heart of the United States. The ODNI, DCIA, SIS—

British Secret Intelligence Service [formerly MI-6]–and the Mossad, all agreed with the new piece of breaking news that the statements of the Dear Leader were based more on fact than bluster than ever before.

Fourth, The Islamic Republic of Iran, made a report almost identical to North Korea's regarding thermonuclear weapons and delivery systems. The report came from the usually reliable state news outlets, IRIB [*Islamic Republic of Iran Broadcasting*], *Iran, Ettelaat, Kayhan, Hamshahri, Resalat,* and *Iran Daily* and *Tehran Times* [which are both English language papers.], as well as *Al Jazeera*.

It was as if President Daniels had pulled four rabbits out of a hat simultaneously so far as voters' allegiances went. the DPRK national and free world news outlets changed in a week from being almost uniformly in opposition of policies and history of the president. The tune changed to, "we can't switch horses in the middle of the stream" with war looming. It was almost unanimously agreed that the tough genius in the White House had to stay on to guide the nation through another existential crisis (or two, or three).

In what seemed like a divine wand had waved over the president and the White House, her favorability rating soared to 80% in favor—including both political parties. If it was a miracle, Sybil was willing to accept it.

She almost had time to savor the change, because she had to meet with the world's best military officers and the Congress, to find an area of agreement on how to deal with the foreign threat. Was a pre-emptive threat on the short list?

CHAPTER
EIGHT

I n the short run—despite the incredibly great importance for the long run—Sybil's attention had to be
divided almost equally between military strategy meetings with the JCOS and large but equally secret conferences with Canadian and Mexican authorities who were
largely in favor of creating a massive new country—to
be named The United States of North America with its
capital in Washington DC. That much had been agreed
upon among the three currently existing countries, but
not much else. There was an enormity at stake.

The conferences—called the North American
Union—meetings were rotated among the major cities
of the three countries over the first six months on a
fairly frequent basis. In the second meeting—held in
Ottawa—several important preliminary elements of
this huge undertaking were decided. All three national
leaders—US President Sybil Norcroft Daniels, Canadian
Premier Justin Pierre James Trudeau, and Mexican

President Andrés Manuel López Obrador became friends after the third month of talks and were on first name basis privately. Sybil was especially pleased about that because she was sure they could use that friendship to break down hurdles and barriers.

The problems were serious, and at their third meeting they agreed to an agenda to list and to come to understand the problems in each country that could prove to be impediments to forming a union. To get at this thorny set of issues, they agreed to include—from each country—leaders in a large number of disparate subsets of their populations. In equal proportions, all three countries invited lawmakers, military officers, police officers, union leaders, successful business-people, university professors, grade school principals, farmers and agribusiness people, leaders of the entertainment industry, financial leaders, social workers, athletic directors, statisticians, and diplomats.

In an absolutely closed-door session, President Daniels went first. She listed, then expanded on a wide variety of problems—some of which were widely known from the global news services and some were held closer to the vest of the people in the know in the nation. The list included: restive racial relations, inner city and rural poverty, decaying infrastructure, the great ideological and political divide in the country, racism, xenophobia, crime, the colossal national debt, student debt, unequal and extremely expensive health care, police abuse of minorities, governmental corruption, the declining dollar, the mounting interest in secession, and the challenges of dealing with the hostile nations of the Middle East, Iran, North Korea, China, and Russia.

It took Sybil and a dozen experts to give thumbnail sketches of each problem in its turn. To assist her two new friends, Sybil had her people hand out a succinct but well thought out and candid White Paper. By the time she concluded, the three leaders were fatigued and more than a little disheartened. It was time for lunch for three responsible statespersons who had lost their appetites.

After lunch it was siesta time, then President Obrador's turn to try and inspire the group.

President Obrador sighed as he readied himself to present the list of Mexico's problems: religion—entrenched Catholics versus all other religions (talk about thorny ideological divide), poverty (poverty, poverty), governmental corruption, the US border wall and the plethora of background issues surrounding it, racism (European-Mexicans v. indigenous peoples v. Mestizos), and inculcated indifference to getting problems solved.

He touched on xenophobia and distrust of the United States. President Obrador spoke candidly about mutual problems shared by the US and Mexico, such as corruption and criminality and expanded on the deplorable health care statistics, the age-old and seemingly unsolvable haves v. the have-nots divide, illiteracy, entrenched superstitions, suspicion of science and other nonreligious thinking (also mentioned by President Daniels with regards the situation in the US with the far-right wingers and the far-left wingers), corruption and criminality in their election processes, determination by both the haves, the have-nots, the political incumbents, and the entrenched Catholics, to preserve the status quo, air pollution, management of sewage, danger of extinction of cherished species, the smuggling of chemical fluids, which end up spilling into the rivers, lakes, and beaches (compounded by the finding that the inhabitants of Mexico have high levels of lead and cadmium in the blood, which results in high rates of kidney and stomach disease and cancer), crime and the drug gangs (and their inordinate level of power), over population (complicated by ignorance about birth-control or religious proscription against it), and Japanese fishing trawlers upsetting the biosystems of the ocean by harvesting sharks for their fins despite agreeing not to do so (which is also complicated by a high level of indebtedness to Japan which is used as leverage against the struggling Mexican government).

"*Heavy sigh,*" was the unspoken response to President Obrador's litany of horrors when he finally—and thankfully–resumed his seat.

Prime Minister Trudeau lightened the mood a little by laughing and saying, "I bet you can hardly wait until tomorrow morning when I get to tell you all about Canada's dirty little secrets."

Secretary of State Beverly Armont Willardson and the members of the Western Asia and the Middle East desk attended the AMEN [Association of Middle Eastern Nations] annual meeting held in Tehran. AMEN is a sub-association of the ECO [The Economic Cooperation Organization an Asian political and economic intergovernmental organization which was founded in 1985 in Tehran by the leaders of Iran, Pakistan, and Turkey, which, in turn, is under the United Nations]

Each year the meeting was held in a different country, and each year that country took advantage to gouge the attendees financially, and to pummel them ideologically. The Islamic Republic of Iran took full advantage of its opportunity.

The opening welcome and keynote speech was given by President Hassan Rouhani. When Secy. Willardson reported back to President Daniels, his summation of the five-day meeting was:

"Madam President, the other attendees and I listened to a mind numbing five-hour tirade against the United States. Most of it was the usual scripted 'Great Satan' litany, but there was a new theme—presumably coming from the Grand Ayatollah Khamenei himself. He announced a new bi-lateral treaty and military association with his 'great friend and fellow sufferer' Kim Jong Un.

Rouhani flatly declared, that the two nations—the IRI, and the DPRK—will shortly drive the Great Satan and Little Satan [Israel] off the face of the earth with the intervention of Allah and His great "Day of Judgment," known as Yawm al-Qiyāmah lightening'. This came after a very lengthy denunciation of the actions of the United States since well before the emergence of the Islamic State under its founder Ayatollah Ruhollah Khomeini and ended with a prosecutorial type statement of charges under Sharia and international law."

"Specific threats?"

"Not quite. They use code when they want to reference nuclear bombs: 'End of Days', 'Yawm al-Qiyāmah', 'Day of Judgment', that sort of thing. There was some muttering in the crowd that he was talking about fiery missiles, great explosions, etc. In my opinion, it was about as direct as they ever get. I pretty much think that this is a genuine threat and an intended escalation, Madam President."

"Have you received anything from the DPRK about this more formal relationship with the IRI?"

"Not yet, but the Swiss desk gave us a heads-up to watch for incoming."

"Bombs or messages?" Sybil asked with a small chuckle.

"The latter, I hope."

That was one more head scratcher in a day full of them.

Prime Minister Trudeau took the podium at 3:30 in the afternoon with his presentation of his country's problems:

"Here's Canada's list: toxic dumps, air pollution (smog, acid rain, oilsands carbon emissions, and transboundary pollution), systemic racism in African Nova Scotia with serious health consequences, underrepresentation of indigenous people and people of color in elective bodies across the board, noncompliance in provincial nursing care facilities, inefficiency and slowing of the economy, rising taxes, declining value of the Canadian dollar, poverty (especially among minorities), declining postal services, and third world conditions in minority sections of the country.

"Canada has transitioned to living in a media echo chamber, ignoring "the other side", lack of jobs in the Maritimes, laws the have killed off export of Canadian energy with consequent loss of income for Canada's social problems and Infrastructure. There is mistrust of each region of the country by the others and interprovincial disagreements, low population, and now more frequent failures of the salmon fish farms on the coasts.

"They concentrate hundreds of thousands of fish in floating farms using open net pens. The farms breed pests and diseases like Infectious Salmon Anemia, sea lice, and Piscine Reovirus, and can pass those on to wild populations, core housing needs, and refugee issues management. And... I might add, that there is a proposed new nation called Cascadia which says it is going to take a whack out of Western Canada to unite with California and Oregon.

"It is our understanding that your Supreme Court has given it a go-ahead. And, the North Koreans call you hegemonists! they have nothing going on like Canada does," he said with a hearty laugh.

"Justin, that is my worst nightmare. I hope all the systems in Canada have better sense than we do."

"Not that it needs saying, but Canada has made the idea of secession clear both times Quebec tried. We are not going to give the secessionists in our country the time of day."

"Good for you, My Friend."

As if to add punctuation to Justin Trudeau's comment, satellite data within the hour recorded two missiles being fired by North Korea. The missile landed in the DPRK's own territory this time. On the Korean Peninsula there are exotic sand dunes along the coast with beach dunes reach up to forty meters above sea level. The missiles landed in Haeju, North Korea. President Daniels and her government were well aware of the area because hundreds of cargo ships were being filled with sand every day for sale around Western Asia in direct contravention of United Nations sanctions. The valuable sand was then transferred to other ships at sea to avoid the prying eyes of customs officials.

President Daniels shared that item of intel with her two friends during the evening dinner in Ottawa and added acerbically, "I guess you might just as well add that to our already long list of drawbacks."

"Frankly, I was glad to learn that both the US and Canada have thorny problems to deal with. I was afraid our desire to unite our three countries into one big one would be dead in the water as soon as I spoke up about Mexico's issues."

Trudeau said, "I think we need to look on all of these problems as part of our problems here in the United States of North America."

"Amen to that," said the two other leaders.

The ultimate pragmatist, Sybil, said, "So, let's get started on a plan to work on solutions, not just wringing our hands over our problems."

The following day, the three leaders and their staffs had developed an agenda, agreed on the next meeting place (Mexico DF) in three months, and a scientific assessment of the problems that would make a union impractical and unsellable to their separate constituencies. That same day, Sybil met with the director of the infrastructure rebuilding, Devon Greyshire, and the Speaker of the House Shirley Mair Zimbrowski, and received good news of real progress for one bright spot in the day.

"We will finish New York and New Jersey next week, and probably have the entire eastern seaboard completed before Christmas."

"You are ahead of schedule, you two. Congrats. Are you also under budget?"

Speaker Zimbrowski grinned from ear to ear.

"That's the best part. We have so many donators and so many private businesses involved, that we will not have to use government funds for another half a year at the earliest, even if all our donations dry up between now and then."

"And that won't happen, right?" Sybil asked.

"Not a chance," Greyshire said, "Our problem is to vet all the private contractors who are willing to put up the front money on valid projects. This is a jubilee kind of year, and almost everyone is catching the fever."

"Not to put a damper on anything, but what about theft, fraud, and other criminal activity?"

"Minor, and we have caught almost every crook who made a try. Talking about volunteers; we have a small army of lawyers working pro bono, retired cops and federal agents to provide security, and a cracker-jack team of CPAs to keep us all on the straight and narrow. We are on a roll, Madam President. This project... this mission… can't fail, short of war or the Yellowstone Crater blowing its cork."

"Don't anyone mention 'war' for fear of jinxing everything," Sybil said, only half joking.

What the president knew that neither Greyshire nor Zimbrowski knew, was that representatives of the US and of the DPRK had been meeting in Geneva for the past two years to come to settlements that would let the world heave a weary sigh of relief, and allow sanctions to be removed from the pitiful and suffering people of North Korea. The results had been mediocre—to say the least—thus far.

CHAPTER
NINE

The Supreme Court began its new year–as it always did–on the first Monday in November. The chief justice had approved a very difficult and ambitious agenda for himself and the other eight justices. There were four secession cases, a challenge to Roe v. Wade, two different police/minority relations reform cases, another attempt by Kansas to allow a slightly altered definition of evolution by a divine creator to be taught in high schools (over the objections of almost every scientist and scientific organization).

There was also a case to determine whether or not it was lawful to set up conversation teams of African-American/Latino neighborhood leaders, police, and university professors (conspicuously leaving the usual strutters and self-aggrandizers out), with authority just below those of city and county councils. That was the brainchild of President Daniels.

Sybil had been determined to avoid a race riot or race related riots throughout the country which had been the nemesis of several previous administrations. So, she decided to pursue a two-pronged long-term plan to avoid them. First, she made a personal call to her vice-president.

"Gifford, How are you doing?"

"All right, Madam President; and how're you?"

"Busy as a one-armed paper hanger. I suspect you are getting bored with your situation as vice-president. Every veep I ever met was."

"May I speak candidly, Madam President?"

"Please do."

"I am absolutely bored stiff. Whoever invented this job had a real cruel streak. I would love to serve, really serve."

"I was hoping you would. I have a huge and important job for you, one that will likely last through both terms of this presidency, if I get re-elected."

"You've got me hooked."

"You are uniquely qualified to head up a nationwide program to handle the race problems in the country. African-Americans v. police, newcomers of color v. entrenched nativists and people who have been here a while and don't want anyone else to come in. Part of this will be to study racism in law enforcement systems and to root out the bad apples or even the bad apple departments.

"I want you to learn all there is to know about the concepts of defunding or even deleting some departments. Big changes have happened before—check-out Camden, New Jersey and see how their plan is working out. On a federal level, I will not tolerate racism in the slightest; however, I don't want any sort of wholesale attack on good agents or police just because they are white. Investigate the concept of racism committed by people, particularly law enforcement people who are not Caucasian.

"I have been mulling over a plan since I was the DCIA and talked it over with the veep at the time and with President Willets. They liked it and thought it was worth a try. I want you to go to every state and territory, every big city and lots of small ones and develop a groundswell movement to establish committees made up of good cops, reasonable neighborhood leaders, university students of police and inner city citizen issues, lawyers, financial whizzes and city planners.

Come up with some sort of plan to put young black men back to work even if they have criminal records. Find a way to move the young people most vulnerable to recruitment away from the ghettos and into smaller, safer, more productive places to life. Find how to make a system of safe houses for girls where they can enjoy their lives without harassment. Get anti-racism, pro-police, classes going for the neighborhoods and vice versa—also for the cops.

"If I left anything out, you think of it. Whatever is needed; you get it done."

"All by myself?" Vice-President de Luca asked with a slightly mischievous grin.

Sybil raised an eyebrow, and they both laughed.

"Of course not, Gifford. In fact, you are honest; and I trust you. You will have all but a bottomless treasury and blank checks to draw from. You are a good man and a good businessman. You are about as popular in the African-American communities as anyone I have ever known. Get the best people to work with you, preferably people of color, but not entirely so. We have to get blacks and whites talking and working together. We don't need or want show-boaters. We don't want any cults of personality or use of positions in this program to get power or money. You are a big, intimidating man. Use that as you need to."

"When do I start?"

"Yesterday morning early and do it on the run. Thanks, Gifford."

At four-thirty that afternoon, Sybil attended the largest of her day's meetings. She had planned this meeting ever since the nation had had to quell an outright insurrection. She felt beholdened to the hand selected law enforcement officers—all 3,000 of them– in the auditorium of the Ronald Reagan Building and International Trade Center. The officers were a little overcrowded, and there was some last-minute shuffling and rearranging to get everyone seated.

Sybil was introduced, then, she walked promptly to the podium.

"Ladies and gentlemen–my trusted officers of the law for this great nation—I have come here today to enlist your help in changing something in the country that it is not working well enough. I am sure most of you have worked in law enforcement long enough to have dealt with a race riot. There have been too many of them at too great a cost in money, property, lives, morale, and ill-will. You know me for being candid. I never place blame on someone else for something I have done.

"We have come to what appears to be an ideological impasse on several levels and between several different types of issues. Racism and race relations have assumed an inordinately severe degree of mistrust and failure of cooperation. Police have been unfair, brutal, and even murderous. The minority communities are regularly rude and uncooperative, and much too often violent in their dealings with law enforcement. We are all citizens of the United States and should be enjoying its promise, or at least striving to make our society one in which everyone enjoys the same opportunity to pursue legitimate happiness.

"We will start anew from this day forward. Now–as officers of the law–we will not be racists, will not tolerate those who are; and we will behave in the fashion of the motto on our vehicles; to protect and serve. There are brutal policemen and women. It is time they found a new career. It is past time that you tolerate them or create a "blue shield".

Now, our daily activities are different; we are responsible not only for our own behavior but for all the other officers we witness and work with. We will report misbehavior, even our own. Everyone makes mistakes. Due process will still be in effect. Your police unions are not going to be interfered with in carrying out defense for you and working to achieve better conditions.

"I am asking for your support. Make new rules; keep them; teach your fellow officers to do the same; and be proactive in getting rid of the bad apples. Don't be coy. You know who they are. You know about ongoing or past sexual harassment. That stops as of now. Eyes open; report to command or IA; bear witness. You do not need to work with that kind of ilk. No woman should be treated that way, should feel unappreciated, or to live in fear in her work-place. That will no longer be tolerated. No more 'wink, wink, nod, nod, look the other way'. If your behavior is within the law, decent, and honorable, you will be fine. If you are doing harm to the force, to your fellow officers, and/or the community, God help you. I won't.

"Furthermore, I am asking you to take part in the new community policing programs that will be sweeping the country shortly. Sit with the good people of the communities in their meeting halls, churches, and on their stoops. Listen and learn; be an example; and teach them to help and not to hinder. Teach them to report crime and their fears of gangs. Help them to help themselves. We must do better than we have done. We must find ways to guide the misinformed or brainwashed victims of gangsters to realize the benefits of being citizens again. Help ex-cons to find gainful employment. I could go on and on, but you get the picture. We all need to help each other."

As soon as she returned to her seat, the Chief of Police of Washington DC took Sybil's place and explained how the workshops were going to take place, where the maps of the large centers were to be found, who the teachers were (including what came as something of a shock, but all the attendees were going to be teachers to share their experiences, talents, and insights), and what was expected of them as students and as student-teachers.

The conference and its workshops went on for three very full days. There were tests, questions asked of both students and teachers in the classrooms, and guest lecturers such as former gang bangers, drug dealers, and ex-cons. Blacks taught blacks taught whites taught blacks and Latinos. Each attendee was required to fill out an objective evaluation of the conference, its teachers, and its teaching methods. Space was left for any and all attendees to gripe, get things off their chests, and to make constructive suggestions.

Sybil had planned the day well and to her advantage. This was to be a family night for the First Family. Cerisse and Drake had done the planning along with the butler and the Executive Residence chef. By presidential order, no one was allowed to wear a tie, a jacket, or a shirt with a collar. No skirts, dresses, or shoes. The menu–while rather informal—was nevertheless all a gourmand could want.

The menu was printed with the occasion being an "unbirthday" celebration for every family member, listed by name. Sybil had ordered sweets to start; but just a taste, she insisted with a wry smile.

Dolley Madison muffins

YIELD: 4-5 dozen
James Madison Waverly Jumbles
(baked donuts)
YIELD: 5 dozen
George Washington's Morning Corn Cakes.
YIELD: 20 med. cakes Theodore Roosevelt's Birthday Cake
YIELD: 5-6 servings

INGREDIENTS:

4 eggs, beaten
2 1/2 cups sugar
1 cup veg oil
1 tbsp cinnamon
5 cups flour
1 qt buttermilk
3 cups raisin bran cereal 1 lb flour
½ lb butter
¾ lb light brown sugar, packed
2 free range eggs
2 cups stone-ground or self rising cornmeal. white or yellow
1 1/2 –2 cups luke-warm water.
1 pkg dry yeast (¼ oz.)

1 cup butter, 1½ cups sugar, 3 well-beaten eggs, 1 cup cold black coffee, 2 cups white flour, ½ cup cocoa, ½ tsp salt

½ tsp cinnamon, 2 tbsps rose water, pre-heat oven to 350°. 6 tbsps sugar or brown sugar, 8 tsps baking powder, 4 tsps salt, 4 eggs, 3 cups milk or buttermilk, ¾ cup canola oil

½ tsp vanilla, 1 tsp baking soda, 1 tbsp vinegar,

Ready in 30 mins	Ready in 45 mins
Ready in 25 mins	Ready in 40 mins

DIRECTIONS:

Mix all ingredients together in very large bowl In a large bowl, cream butter & sugar until light brown in color.

Beat in the eggs Mix all ingredients in large bowl, do not overmix Preheat oven to 350°. Grease and dust 8 X 8 cakepan with cocoa.

Let the batter stand in refriger-ator > 24 hrs before baking Then, add rose-water, gradually stir in the flour. Chill the dough for 1-2 hours Let mix sit for 5 mins. Cream butter & add sugar a little at a time

Bake for 20 min in a 400° oven

The batter keeps for 4 weeks and can be sectioned off for repeated bakings. Pinch off a piece of dough at a time & roll into 2" rope. Join the rope ends together to form a ring. Bake the Jumbles for 10-12 mins in center of oven Pour about ¾ cup of batter on med. hot greased griddle. Fry until bubbles appear, then turn over. Fry until golden brown. Cream well, add eggs, sift flour, salt, soda, & cocoa 3 times, Add coffee to batter altern-ating with flour mixture

> Cool on wire rack then serve or store in air-tight container for up to a week. Then, add vinegar and vanilla. Bake at 350°~30-40 mins.

In keeping with the historical presidential theme, supper was Thomas Jefferson's favorite: rice soup, round of beef, turkey, mutton, ham, loin of veal, cutlets of mutton or veal, fried eggs, fried beef, a pie called macaroni, which appeared to be a rich crust filled with scallion onions or shallots to visitors. The number of dishes was immense, but the portions were small. Besides, the two children were not overly keen about the rice soup or shallots; but they devoured the macaroni pie and left room for more presidential baked dessert items. They went to bed with full bellies and heads full of Grandma's stories. The entire family had one of their first real undisturbed sleeps since the presidency began.

The morning started at dawn's first light with an impromptu wrestling match. By a long time agreement, big Charles played the role of a hemiplegic when he wrestled his petite wife, who always seemed to win—one of those cherished little traditions that provides the glue that keeps a marriage together. Once they had all showered and combed their unruly hair, the stewards brought in a huge breakfast. In keeping with the historical theme, this breakfast—per Grandma's order—was a faithful copy of Nellie Grant's Wedding Breakfast Menu, May 21, 1874, in the State Dining Room: Woodcock and Snipe on Toast, Soft Crabs on Toast, Chicken Croquettes with Fresh Peas, Aspic of Beef Tongue, Lamb Cutlets Broiled Spring Chicken, Strawberries with Cream, white cake iced with doves, roses, and ships bells, Ice Creams and Ices, Fancy Cup Cakes, Punch, Coffee, or Hot Chocolate.

The children refused even to taste the aspic, stating that they did not like it.

"Have you ever tasted it?" Cerisse asked the boys.

"No."

"Then, how do you know you don't like it?"

"Because," which is the irrefutable rebuttal of all children, and it ended the argument.

They tried a bite or two of everything else and three or four of the strawberries, white cake, ice creams and ices, cupcakes, and hot chocolate. It was a successful breakfast.

Neither boy threw up, and their father, Drake told three jokes designed for children that made everyone laugh in a soul-restoring manner.

Then the red phone rang.

Sybil picked up the receiver and said, "Lioness." Then, she said, "I'm on my way."

On her way along the corridor from the residence to the Situation Room, Navy Lt. Brice Campbell, the new officer in charge carried the nuclear football and walked one step behind the sober and determined president.

CHAPTER
TEN

The mood in the Situation Room was grim. Everyone present stepped away from his or her seat and stood at attention—even the civilians—as President Daniels, her body guard, and the NSA officer carrying the "football", entered the room.

"Please be seated, ladies and gentlemen. Who is going to give the sitrep?"

Everyone but General Glen Gabler, Sr., the CJCS, sat down.

"Madam President, here is the short of it. A US Navy patrol boat with fifty-six souls aboard was attacked by an Iranian navy destroyer. They fired two C-802 Noor anti-ship missiles. These are an Iranian development of a Chinese weapon. We waited a bit to inform you until naval intelligence could confirm the attack, its source, the type of weapon, and whether or not our ship was in international waters.

"The USS Guadalcanal went down with all hands. They were in international waters. We have their GPS unit and exact GPS coordinates at the time the ship was killed. Their mission was routine—no hostile provocations, either intentionally or by accident; and this was not a spy ship, nor was it a spy mission. We have satellite video images of the attack. It came from the DPRK Sahand Class Destroyer, Kim Jong Un Lightening, an entirely new design of their navy; and the first of its kind to be launched, so far as we know."

The room became silent as President Daniels templed her fingers on the bridge of her nose—her habit when she was concentrating deeply.

She looked around the room at the intent and deeply concerned faces, then said in her iciest and most determined quiet voice, "Any doubts, General?"

"None."

"Is the evidence ready for transmission to the UN?"

"Way ahead of you, Ma'am."

"To the Russians and the Red Chinese?"

"We left that for your decision; so, you can determine our course and how much you want to share with the hostiles."

"Send it now. I will call the leaders as soon as this meeting is over."

"I hate even to say, Madam President," the CJCS said, "but the ball is in your court. What are your orders?"

There was no hesitation. Sybil had made all her decisions during her three minutes of private thought.

"Take out every Iranian ship you can find, as fast as you can find them. Kill them whether they are moored, in dry dock, in Iranian waters, or anywhere at sea. Look for coal barges transferring coal against the UN sanctions. Find partially finished ships in their naval construction sites. Kill them. When that is all done, report to me; and then—and only then—will I communicate with the Supreme Leader of the Democratic Peoples' Republic of Korea. I hope I have made myself clear. Any questions, General Gabler?"

"No, Ma'am. Lima Charlie [roughly, 'loud and clear']. We already have our secret squirrels on the ground and are monitoring the area with the eye in the sky every ten seconds. We are ready for now." He thought a moment, "Shall I order carriers?"

"Yes, make it three. Have them park in Iranian waters bristling with nastiness."

"Aye, aye, Ma'am."

The room sounded like a hive of wasps as fingers flew on computers and orders were swiftly conveyed in monotones to points all over the United States and the world as President Daniels left the room.

She arranged for Ultra Top Secret calls to be made from her to Chairman Xi Jinping, and President Vladimir Putin. The message was terse, to the point and devoid of comradely warmth.

"This is the president of the United States. Over the past night, the Democratic Peoples' Republic of Korea sank a United States ship without provocation killing everyone aboard. We have turned away from a great many attacks from that rogue nation. We will not do so this time. As soon as I hang up, you will receive a detailed set of evidence regarding the attack, and a list of what we are doing about it at this moment. Please understand, that this does not and need not affect your countries. However, do not underestimate the level of our wrath. The rogue nation has exceeded even our long-suffering patience. Good day."

She called the leaders of Germany, France, the United Kingdom, Australia, South Korea, and Japan and gave them the same information absent the warnings. She greeted them as "friends and allies."

Two out of the three carrier groups were already in Busan Naval Base in South Korea, and the third was on its way from Yokosuka, Kanagawa, Japan. All of them were at full-speed-ahead with their computerized destination–the naval port of Namp'o in Korea Bay, the port city for Pyongyang. More than once, the ships' captains announced over their loud-speakers that "This is not a drill"; and they did not care a whit if anyone outside their ships heard them. The die was cast.

It is 276 nm from Busan to Namp'o, and the *USS Theodore Roosevelt* and *USS Nimitz* were making forty knots sailing through the night. They were less than two hours out. The *USS Gerald R. Ford,* en route from Yokosuka, was about six hours out. It was intended that the *Gerald R. Ford* would serve as rear guard.

Despite the formidable appearing collection of North Korean forces along the northern shore of the Taedong River–15 km east of the river's mouth—the audacious Americans pulled into battle positions at the mouth of the Taedong River at two bells of the morning watch facing the military port and dropped their fore and aft anchors as if to announce a long and entrenched stay and their obvious intention to blockade the port. The port and its city Namp'o, was a center for the DPRK shipbuilding industry.

North of the city were facilities for freight transportation, aquatic products, and fishery, and a sea salt factory—all regarded as targets, as were their people.

Early risers reported the unauthorized and menacing presence of the two carrier groups, and later risers were treated to the majestic hulk of the *Gerald R. Ford* and its satellite ships on patrol in Korea Bay.

A signal man who was informed, acted reflexively–as the Dear Leader would have wanted–and pushed the panic button. A squadron of Russian MIGs took off from the airport, and US Navy Boeing F/A-18E/F Super Hornets, Lockheed Martin F-35B/C Lightning II, and Boeing MQ-25 Stingrays lifted off the carriers' decks and met the North Koreans' attack.

A very short dog-fight ensued; and every MIG was downed. No American planes or personnel were damaged or killed. AF-A-18F VFA 102 Super Hornets and Lockheed Martin F-35 Lightning IIs–an American family of single-seat, single-engine, all-weather stealth multirole combat aircraft–currently stationed in Busan passed over the then quiet battle zone and tipped their wings to their navy pilot comrades.

The North Korean signalman's press of the panic switch also triggered the approach of what looked like the *USS Nimitz* coming down the Taedong River from above the city. It disappeared as if it were made of paper.

It was later proved to be very much the case: it was a faux ship with considerable technical accuracy holding sixteen replica F-18s, except it was about half the size of the Nimitz, and the planes were identified as fakes before the US attack even commenced.

CNO Dwight Halverson sent terse orders, somewhat outdated even upon arrival: "Commence firing at will in accordance with POTUS order."

Air force jet bombers and their defending fighters began sweeping the country of North Korea from coast to coast and top to bottom in a gridiron pattern taking out hundreds of bases with their facilities and their parked planes—not a few of which were old biplanes. Naval construction centers, raw materials and ammunition dumps, and command and control facilities were damaged beyond repair.

It was doubtful if any individual among the populace or within the government of the DPRK made reference to the United States as a "paper tiger". The attack was as well planned and executed as the Japanese attack on Pearl Harbor on December 7, 1942. But this tiger attack on a much larger target area was accomplished in less time than it took the Japanese and resulted in a great deal more destruction. Fewer civilians were killed or injured than in that historical Japanese surprise attack, and the surprise was every bit as complete.

Before the vaunted North Korean military had a chance to react effectively, the DPRK bombers returned to Busan, and that was not particularly relevant since their capacity to return fire was so effectively reduced. Kim

Jong-un was asleep in his sumptuous bed in the Kumsusan Palace of the Sun when the American attack started, and no one was able to communicate with the palace because that section of Pyongyang happened to be having one of its frequent power outages. The message he received came from the head of his palace guard.

"Field Marshal and Supreme Leader Kim, I regret to awaken you at this hour [it was 0630], but a situation has arisen, Sir. The information is incomplete, but it is certain that, over night, the fiendish Americans and their lackies, the so-called 'South Koreans' have launched an attack all across the country. It appears that mainly naval weaponry and installations have been damaged."

"I have questions, and you had better have answers, young man!" Kim growled. "What is the level of the damage? How many of our dear citizens and military heroes have been killed or injured? And what death and destruction did our heroic forces inflict on the monsters from the West?"

The guard stammered, "The information is still coming in, Supreme Leader… but the damage to our country was severe. Our navy… could… I mean, possibly is… unable to mount either a defense or a return attack. The facilities attacked are likely to be out of commission for years, and the cost—estimated by the admirals—is in the billions of Korean Peoples' won. That is an… early estimate, Great Sir. The admirals also report that the loss of life was not heavy—perhaps a few hundred people, definitely less than a thousand. Our base in Namp'o was completely destroyed, and all its jet fighters and pilots were destroyed in the early hours of last night."

"Tell me the terrible losses suffered by the fiends from the West. How many thousands of men? How many destroyed airplanes? How many large ships sunk?"

"I, I, I, don't have full information, Great Sir. It is early in the battle, say our admirals."

"No one can lie to me. No one can keep things from me. If I learn that you have, your head will roll along with the cowards in our defense forces who failed us. Do you understand, young man?"

"P,p,perfectly, Supreme Leader. The information I have received and hesitated to give you was that no damage to men, ships, or planes of the enemy."

For the next five minutes, the guard heard a rattling tirade laced with every profanity, obscenity, and curse, that he had ever heard plus a few more streaming from the Dear Leader. Then Kim cut off the call.

Kim's next communications were with the admirals still alive in Namp'o and Pyongyang.

To each, Kim screamed almost unintelligibly; but they got the gist. "Heads were going to roll; traitors will pay dearly; anyone who allows information to pass beyond the senior officers or to the international news media will be considered a traitor."

Unlike many other times that Chairman Kim had ventilated, this time the recipients were genuinely more frightened of him than they were of the Americans or of the South Koreans. And—unlike on previous occasions—nearly two dozen of them gathered up their families and headed for the obscure hideaways they had set up in Northeast North Korea, near the Chinese border.

The always reliable asset in the highest Korean echelons reported the news to the American ODNI at serious peril to his own existence. He reported that: the destruction had essentially paralyzed whatever navy the country had, and it would not be a factor for years. A purge had begun among the higher echelon of the military—not just from the navy— and was going to be the equal of Stalin's purge of officers in the '30s. That would further weaken the ranks, efficacy, and morale of the Hermit Kingdom's defense systems.

The nation's military members were operating—or not—in a what could only be described as a state of panic. And, finally, Chairman Kim and his retinue of guards was making a secret tour of the DPRK's missile and nuclear facilities. All bets were off about what he would do. No one in the country, except possibly his sister could carry on a sensible conversation with the man. There even a few furtive whispers about a coup.

President Daniels and her people decided to adopt a wait-and-see attitude about what might happen next and what her response would be. In effect, the highest echelon of American government was holding its collective breath.

CHAPTER
ELEVEN

There was a conspicuous silence coming from the DPRK, including an abrupt cessation of the secret talks that had been taking place in Geneva. The Swiss legation tried and failed to communicate with Kim or anyone else on the government. North Korean communication outlets went black. All avenues were cut off. The American and other western media were the only outlets to describe what had gone on in North Korea, and much of what they had to say was in error—error that no one in the administration took any effort to correct.

Sybil's first insight into the murkiness enveloping Pyongyang came not from North Korea, but from the Mossad. Their information had the objectivity of a video that had been secretly taken of Iran's Supreme Leader speaking to the Iranian Majles [also The Islamic Consultative Assembly]. Preceded by chanting by the assembly members of "Death to America; Death to the Great Satan," the Supreme Leader roundly condemned the United States, Saudi Arabia, and Israel, for "an unprovoked and Jewish type of attack on the peace loving North Korean people."

He described the destruction as the same thing that happened to Hiroshima when peace loving Japanese people were slaughtered. The video obtained by courageous deep-cover Mossad agents lasted almost two hours, but Sybil lost interest after forty-five minutes of lecture on the similarities of this attack to the attack on the Prophet by the villainous Jewish tribe. Her attention returned when the Leader declared,

"We stand with our brethren and all oppressed peoples. The day has come for the great Satan to be conquered and bound for all eternity. Our powerful missiles will fly along with those of our brethren, and the Great Satan will be no more. We will deal with their lackeys, the Little Satan, and the Kingdom of Evil in the desert once we have cut off the head of the serpent."

The references were clear but somewhat difficult to take at face value since the Supreme Leader had made nearly the same threats multiple times in the past; although, usually such threats were aimed at Israel and the Jews of New York.

A week later, a single addition of each of the twelve permitted newspapers contained an empty front page except for a single banner headline stretched across the top of the page of the main four of the principal newspapers and four of the twenty major periodicals, all published in strict obedience in Pyongyang: *Rodong Sinmun* [Labor Daily, published by the Central Committee of the WPK],

Joson Inmingun [Korean People's Army Daily], *Minju Choson* [Democratic Korea, government organ] and *Rodongja Sinmun* [Workers' Newspaper]

It read:

REVENGE SHALL BE OURS SAYS OUR DEAR LEADER.
AMERICA SHALL SHORTLY SEE DEATH COME FROM THE SKIES.
OUR FRIENDS HAVE COME TO OUR AID!!!

The exact same message streamed from all five major television stations of the official network, KCNA, which regularly attracts the attention of the international news media. On the television, the message was repeated several times an hour for a day narrated by the clear young voice of a girl accompanied by background patriotic music. The same message by the same narrator was heard over and over again on the Pyongyang FM Station, Voice of Korea; and the Korean Central Broadcasting Station.

The older American generals said that was altogether reminiscent of Stalin's and Hitler's propaganda in the late 1930s when they were about to invade Poland. Every senior leader of the military and the administration unanimously agreed that the president should take Kim and Khamenei seriously and that she should warn the country.

Reluctantly, Sybil booked airtime on all the television outlets that evening and told them the truth about the North Korean's having sunk a peaceful US Navy ship, and about the retaliatory response by the United States. Her address was very brief. It ended with an admonition for the country to prepare for a missile attack from either or both North Korea and Iran. The rest of the evening's entertainment was pre-empted by repeated experts telling the audiences about how to make a 72-hour emergency pack and what kind of foods, medications, and other supplies, they should have. In a matter of minutes, the nation's grocery chains, drug stores, and hardware outlets, were inundated; and their shelves cleared by hoarders. Americans took to their homes much like they did during the recent COVID-19 pandemic.

The JCOS ordered a general military status of DEFCON 3 until further notice and put NORAD to DEFCON 2. All leaves were cancelled, and all DOD and military personnel were ordered to return to and remain at their home bases unless their duties were deemed to be critical elsewhere. The Atlantic fleet began regular and short-range surveillance deployment; four more carrier groups–including the *USS Nimitz* stationed at the Naval Station Norfolk, and the *USS Nimitz* home based at Naval Base Kitsap, Bremerton, Washington, the *USS Kittyhawk* [rescued from intended scrapping], and the USS Kennedy, and two more air force bomber and fighter jet squadrons were sent to South Korea.

Korea Bay was surrounded by US naval vessels and also England's sole carrier, the *HMS Queen Elizabeth*, in full combat mode, thereby creating a de facto siege status. For the first time in the history of UN sanctions against the DPRK, sanction orders were obeyed to the fullest. North Korea was being strangled.

For good measure, Sybil ordered two carrier groups to enter the Gulf of Oman, one—*the USS Nimitz*, one of two *Nimitzes* home based at the San Diego Naval Air

Station, North Island–was stationed off the Musundam Peninsula at the narrowest point between the UAE and Iran's Qeshm Island, and the second—the *USS George HW Bush*–took a position near the middle of the Persian Gulf east of Ad-Dammam and Manama which gave it quick access to Iran's Büshehr to the northeast and Kish and Hormozgan to the southeast. The range of the battleship and carrier guns made access to the interior of the Islamic Republic of Iran well within their capabilities. All the ships' missiles were armed for tactical nuclear strikes.

President Norcroft, Vice-president de Luca, CJCS Gabler, the Speaker of the House Zimbrowski, the Majority Leader of the Senate Nichols, the news networks, America's allies, and the people of the Western world, held their collective breaths, prayed, and hoped beyond hope that the president's aggressive posture would ensure that the Hermit Kingdom would retract back into its shell.

To say that Kim Jong-un was intimidated would be the zenith of understatement. However, his fears were less about the United States and its satellite states, and more about the murmurings of dissent and a possible coup from within his military establishment. His reasoning was that he had always been able to bluff the fools in Washington; that they would never launch a real war against his country with China and Russia ready and willing to come to his defense; that his generals and admirals were frightened at the posturing by the United States but not so seriously as to risk their heads in a coup attempt; and that the decadent Westerners were too frightened of having another world war break out if an attack was made on Pyongyang.

According to CIA analysts, and our asset in North Korea, the Dear Leader was wrong in all his assessments and was either delusional or suicidal even to think of launching a missile attack. Iran's Supreme Leader commanded a much better, more experienced, and more determined, military organization. He had his personal doubts, but he had convinced himself that Allah had spoken to him in a dream telling him that he should shed his timidity; now was the time to strike because Iran had a determined ally; and both nations had nukes. A pre-emptive strike would cause such fear to penetrate into the hearts of the kuffars that world domination would come to the Islamic Republic so long as they obeyed Allah. With Allah on their side, they could not fail.

Like his newly acquired best friend, Khamenei kept all his thoughts close to his vest and forbade–on an absolute scale–any leaks to the outside world. The friendship status caused the intensely religious Iranian considerable dyspepsia given the heathen and anti-religious convictions of Kim. He and Chairman Kim nevertheless held another meeting on the first of September, the details of which were never released.

Threats from the two rogue states were not the only issue facing Sybil N. Daniels and the country. The citizens were deeply divided along political ideological lines, and the November elections were only two months away. Sybil's standings in the voters' polls remained stagnant, and it was a case of 'glass half-full or glass have empty' choice for her campaign managers to try and understand and how to spin the information.

Jinx Matterdome, her campaign manager, said that they needed to break the logjam, "What we need in this country is a good war. That always helps the incumbent."

"Bite your tongue, Jinx," the president said smiling.

"Sorry, but I would only say such a thing to the members of the family."

"Beware, families have fallings-out all the time," Sybil said seriously.

"Of course, but we do need to jazz up the race a bit, and in our favor."

"Anything exciting in mind?"

"Not really. But, I do think we need to get you out on the stump touting your victories—like how well you handled the insurrection, the planning and preparation for the next pandemic, the beginnings of real change in the relationships between police and people of color, and how great the repair and refurbishing of the infrastructure is going belong on the short list."

"Politicking, you mean? You know that is not my strong suit, Jinx."

"Nobody likes to floss their teeth, either; but it has to be done."

"Okay, work out a schedule with the Chief of Staff, and get the writers busy putting some speech drafts together. I suppose I am going to have to take my medicine and get out on the stump."

"Oh, Madam President, you are so smart. You figured that all out by yourself!"

Sybil stuck out her tongue at her manager.

"I'll work on all that, Ma'am; but we'll have to concentrate on the swing states with the big electoral college votes. We just won't have time to hit the rest more than with a quickie rabble-rousing hoorah for half day."

"You're right, Jinx. Get me an update by tomorrow— two days max."

"Wilco."

Sybil felt guilty most of the time she was not spending on the secession issues. The several entities were now working from the same game plan, apparently, because they were all making progress through the steps of the justice system, each determined to get their case heard before the Supreme Court. They had a precedent to cite— the Cascadia decision—which would make it far easier to persuade the now softened-up justices.

To Sybil, it was like dominoes falling in slow motion. Alaska, the AIP [Alaska Independence Party]; Texas, the Freedom Texas Movement; the Second Vermont Republic Movement, and the New England Independence Movement were all headed for federal appeals courts; and there did not seem to Sybil that there were any serious stumbling blocks in their way.

All she could do was to dedicate a portion of her stump speeches to a learned argument against secession. Try as she might, she could perceive only a luke-warm reception to her scholarly and impassioned efforts. The polls bore out her concerns. Maybe it was not good politics, she thought; but–good for her reelection or not–she deemed it likely to be the most important issue of her presidency. She positively had to thwart the secessionists' progress.

On October 10, Party Foundation Day in North Korea—an important and mandatory observance—a national holiday in the DPRK, Kim Jong-un started the celebration with a bang heard around the world. He ordered the inter-Korean joint liaison office building in North Korea's Kaesong Industrial Zone, just north of the Demilitarized Zone—the historical and symbolic building where the mutual Kaesong inter-Korean talks were supposed to be held to improve relations and to pursue mutual interests–to be blown to smithereens in a fit of spite because defectors in the ROK released balloons full of papers critical of the Dear and Supreme Leader.

Pyongyang cut all communication channels with the South after telegraphing an announcement of Kim's latest move. The office was established in 2018 at the DPRK's request to foster better ties with South Korea. The building was empty at the time, and there were no casualties.

The question of the day around the civilized world was–simply put—"What's next?"

The world did not have to wait long. Two days later, satellite images obtained by every Western nation revealed that two large ICBMs were fired from desert areas of both countries –outside Pyongyang, North Korea, and from an arid area of Kurdistan, in northern Iran. All four were launched successfully, and all four were quite obviously on a vector towards the United States of America.

CHAPTER
TWELVE

Sybil sat in the somber White House Situation Room where she and most of the others would remain for long hours over the next three days. They watched a bank of television screens in real time. What they looked at was what prime time television warned about: "Be warned that what you are about to see may—and certainly did—contain graphic and violent images. Do not permit children to view these images." Sybil wished every minute of those seventy-two hours that she did not have to view them either.

The first few minutes of images were videos from body cams of marines, sailors, and airmen en route to Korea Bay, North Korea. Another set was on its way to the Gulf of Hormuz with a clear view of the west coast of Iran. A third set showed the progress of huge bombers and their fighter jet defenders eating up the miles to touchdowns 6,500 miles away. Another bank of screens tracked four separate ICBMs on a computed track towards Chicago, New York, Los Angeles, and Dallas, Texas.

The missiles that originated in Iran were identified as the KN-08. NORAD was able to track them in flight; but in open warfare, when the KN-08 was operationally deployed, they were expected be more difficult to defeat than fixed-site missiles because it could be moved around secretly by the North Korean regime to make it more difficult for the U.S. to locate and target preemptively during a crisis. NORAD was almost glad that they were in the air because they could not be hidden from the computers and the computer driven video surveillance.

The existence of the missiles was never questioned; their vectors were computed and recomputed over and over again. The computer readouts and the paths of the large missiles were unerring.

NORAD [North American Aerospace Defense Command] had been involved from the moment of launching of the missiles and was acting out measures which had been part of their daily drills for a decade or more. The system is a combined organization of the United States and Canada that provides aerospace warning, air sovereignty, and protection, for Northern America. Headquarters for NORAD and the NORAD/United States Northern Command [USNORTHCOM] center are located at Peterson Air Force Base in El Paso County, near Colorado Springs, Colorado. They were well prepared for this critical existential threat.

The ANR [Alaskan NORAD Region] through which the ICBMS had to pass maintains continuous capability to detect, validate, and warn off, any atmospheric threat in its area of operations from its Regional Operations

Control Center (ROCC) at Joint Base Elmendorf–Richardson, Alaska. ANR also maintains the readiness to conduct a continuum of aerospace control missions, which include daily air sovereignty in peacetime, contingency and deterrence in time of tension, and active air defense against manned and unmanned air-breathing atmospheric vehicles in times of crisis. This was unanimously agreed to be one of those times of crisis.

ANR is supported by both active duty and reserve units. Active duty forces are provided by 11 AF and the Canadian Armed Forces (CAF), and reserve forces provided by the Alaska Air National Guard. Both 11 AF and the CAF provide active duty personnel to the ROCC to maintain continuous surveillance of Alaskan airspace. There was a seamless hand-off of surveillance responsibility as the missiles streaked into Canadian air space.

Canadian NORAD Region Headquarters is at CFB Winnipeg, Manitoba. It is responsible for providing surveillance and control of Canadian airspace. The Royal Canadian Air Force provides alert assets to NORAD. CANR is divided into two sectors, which are designated as the Canada East Sector and Canada West Sector. Both Sector Operations Control Centers (SOCCs) are co-located at CFB North Bay Ontario. The routine operation of the SOCCs includes reporting track data, sensor status and aircraft alert status to NORAD headquarters. In 1996 CANR was renamed 1 Canadian Air Division and moved to CFB Winnipeg. Both sectors had ICBMs to surveille and the Canadians kept up the stream of intelligence about the flight patterns of the missiles.

Canadian air defense forces assigned to NORAD include 409 Tactical Fighter Squadron at CFB Cold Lake, Alberta and 425 Tactical Fighter Squadron at CFB Bagotville, Quebec. All squadrons fly the McDonnell Douglas CF-18 Hornet fighter aircraft. Ten of the fighters streaked off into the cold sky to intercept the hostile missiles.

Two missiles exploded in mid-air. One over the empty north country of Alberta and the other in northern British Columbia near Prince Rupert and the Peace River. That left two still underway and rapidly passing out of the territory where the Canadian squadrons could get to them. One was confirmed to be headed towards Chicago or perhaps to one of the populous areas further south, and the other missile seemed to be directly online to strike the center of the Greater Dallas area.

Cold Lake and Bagotville communicated that they had taken out two but left two for the Americans at CONR [The Continental NORAD Region].

"Good hunting," said the Bagotville radioman.

The Continental NORAD Region is the component of NORAD that provides airspace surveillance and control and directs air sovereignty activities for CONUS [the Contiguous United States]. CONR is the NORAD designation of the United States Air Force First Air Force/AFNORTH. Its headquarters is located at Tyndall Air Force Base, Florida. The First Air Force (1 AF) is responsible for the USAF air defense mission. It is the United States Air Force component of United States Northern Command (NORTHCOM).

1 AF/CONR-AFNORTH comprises Air National Guard Fighter Wings assigned an air defense mission to on federal orders, made up primarily of citizen airmen. The primary weapons systems are the McDonnell Douglas F-15 Eagle and General Dynamics F-16 Fighting Falcon aircraft.

It plans, conducts, controls, coordinates, and ensures air sovereignty, and provides for the unilateral defense of the United States. It is organized with a combined First Air Force command post at Tyndall Air Force Base and two Sector Operations Control Centers [SOCC] at Rome, New York for the US East ROCC (Eastern Air Defense Sector) and McChord Field, Washington for the US West ROCC [Western Air Defense Sector] manned by active duty personnel to maintain continuous surveillance of CONUS airspace. There is intentional overlap with the Canadian protection units in the northern half of CONUS.

Detection was accomplished for this incident with an ever-growing series of radar installations stretching across the vast reaches of Canada. NORAD's "radar fence" was meant to act as a first line of defense, giving as much advance warning as possible when attack planes or missiles were launched toward the United States or Canada. It was never argued that airplanes alone could stop all intruders. The planes were there to provide time to react with retaliatory missiles and possibly affect some form of evacuation or allow civilians to reach bomb shelters. For Dallas and San Francisco on this occasion, it was presumed that an order to evacuate would only cause panic and would likely cause more death than a missile strike or add to the casualties when the missile hit its target.

The pilots and ground crew had trained endlessly to be able to scramble and take to the air on a moment's notice, and they were very good at it in both countries. It was hoped that the planes could be used to intercept and destroy incoming enemy aircraft, or even take out a missile or two if they were lucky. Incoming missiles could not be dealt with in any practical way by planes.

The missile command generals now stepped in as the missiles were becoming evident to the naked eye and were on target to hit US cities in less than an hour. Those generals were well aware that North Korea also has the ability to marry the missile with a nuclear warhead. But, the US has thirty ground-based interceptors at Fort Greely, Alaska, and Vandenberg Air Force Base, California. The leaders of NORAD and NORTHCOM and the missile command were responsible for launching the interceptors against North Korean missiles since they now threatened the homeland.

The emotional and professional sense of purpose included the fact that some of the officers had homes and families in the two target cities. That went a long way to focus their attentions. With less than half an hour to impact, twenty missiles were about to be launched from both US bases computer and laser focused on two streaks of light hurtling through the sky. The computers handled the physics of the trajectory, but the men and women with their fingers on the "fire" buttons were in control of the time of release.

The tension in the missile control headquarters was electric. The control lieutenants sweat profusely, not quite bleeding at every pore, but severe enough.

Gen. Hoyt Strallings calmly gave the orders to both headquarters, "Fire on my O. Five, four, three, two, one...Fire!"

The explosive launches rocked the military buildings and could be heard for over five miles away. The light display of twenty missiles firing simultaneously was awe-inspiring, even frightening. It was only a few minutes before the television screens in the Situation Room were able to place the twenty v. one light displays on the same screen. It would be only a few seconds before the watchers would know if the NORAD missiles were going to land harmlessly somewhere in the barren stretches of Canada, or if the hostile missiles would disappear in a burst of white-hot flame and acrid smoke. Or... if Chicago and San Francisco would be turned to dust.

Sybil did something she had never done in her life before. She began to bite her nails. She was afraid she was going to cry, or faint, or shriek, and humiliate, herself. Gen. Gabler placed his big hand gently on her forearm without saying a word. Everyone in the Situation Room empathized with their president.

Aboard the *USS Theodore Roosevelt*–still located at the mouth of the Taedong River near the west coast of North Korea, the lead carrier for what was now called Operation EndGameWar–Admiral Trescot received official orders from the CNO, passed down from the CJCS, and ultimately from the Commander-in-Chief keeping the chain of command fully responsible to history.

"Carry out Operation EndGameWar immediately. God be with you."

Trescot stiffened up his spine and radioed encrypted orders to his fellow admirals and ships' captains, "Commence firing per Operation EndGameWar. Out."

In three seconds, the morning sky lit up with hundreds of nuclear weaponized missiles. They all had specific targets—the great majority being important military and governmental installations. Special emphasis was placed on the attacks against, Nanjin Uranium Mine near Vladivostok, Russia, Musan Uranium mine near the Yalu River in northwestern North Korea, Hyesan, Ch'olsin, Kujang, Dandong, Tongrim, Sunch'on, and Wiwon Uranium Mines; Cheonmasan Mining and Milling and Uranium enrichment facility, and Atomic Energy Research Institute located at Bungangjig.

Other primary nuclear and critical military sites Included: Yongbyon nuclear complex, Hagap Underground Nuclear Reprocessing and Enrichment Facility and Explosive Test Site in Gaphyundong, Huicheon, Jagang province Pyongsong. There was considerable concentration by the US missile teams and planes on military educational and research centers: College of Science and College of Gifted Students in Unjong-guyok, Pyongyang, International Chemical Joint Venture Company in Hamhung, South Hamgyong Province, Hamheung University of Chemical Industry and Engineering, Geumho-Jigu Light Water Reactor Site, located in Geumho-Jigu, Sinpo, Hamgyeongnam-do, Taecheon 200MWe Nuclear Power Reactor located in Taecheon-gun, Pyeonganbuk-do, and Punggye-ri Nuclear Test Facility located in Punggye-ri, Gilju-gun, North Hamgyeong Province.

It was known that the DPRK had an estimated thirty-five nuclear warheads and where they were located. Those sites were attacked first and most, except for Dear Leader Kim's residential palace, which ranked in 1st or 2nd place on both the strategic, tactical, and emotional lists of every man and woman with fingers on the triggers.

Besides the nuclear mines and facilities, primary targets included all government buildings and official residences including the Kumsusan Palace of the Sun where the best intelligence said that Kim Jong-un would be that morning. All those targets received nuclear bombardment of one type or size. The USAF and Korean air force from Busan concentrated on military installations, schools, barracks, recreational centers, airports, fields, and hangars, holding what was left of the North Korean air defenses.

What was left of the navy was not worth bothering with other than for the submarines around the carriers to hunt down and destroy the only part of the DRPK navy still in operation. There were known to be a large number of submarines of poor quality, with poor defenses—some lacking sonar and all with weak hulls—which are only able to operate within 30 miles of the North Korean coasts. The submarines were unable make it from one side of the country to the other without refueling. Three hours after the attack began, there were none left.

Admiral Trescot's orders reached the lead carrier in the Persian Gulf within a second of his having pushed the "enter" button on his computer. Admiral Klint Jasperson received the command on the *USS George HW Bush* and took immediate action; action that surprised the officials and people of Iran to death. He motioned with thumbs up to the signalman who had been with him for nearly twenty-five years to commence firing as per the presidential order of EndGameWar. Senior Master Chief O'Leary pushed "enter" on his computer and began barking orders.

No one replied. They did not need to. They set to work in a whir of activity. As happened off the coast of North Korea, Nuclear armed ICBMs and other shorter-range missiles tore open the sky. Several hundreds of them sped towards their pre-programed target sites.

Military and nuclear facilities and high value governmental locations were unaware of the coming of death from the skies. The sites for production of uranium, processing and reprocessing it, submitting it to 50,000 centrifuges, and heavy water reactors, in Karaj, Tehran, Lash-kar Abad, Arak, Qom, Natanz, Esfahan, Anarak, and Büshehr, ceased to be recognizable as buildings, homes, or infrastructure, before lunch.

A mix of regular and nuclear warfare attacks commenced against Supreme Leader Khamenei's residence in Central Tehran–The House of Leadership–on Palestine Street. Around it that were fifty buildings. 500 people were employed at this "Beit Rahbari compound" most recruited from the military and security services. It was considered to be one of the most secure and bombproof buildings on earth. Its most important and secure rooms were below the earth in basements protected by twenty feet of reinforced concrete.

The first bomb to strike the House of Leadership was nuclear, the second a thermite bomb, and the last, a "bunker buster bomb". What was left was a crater. Gone was the Supreme Leader, his wife, his eldest son, seven hundred officers and menial workers, Khamenei's stable of over a hundred horses, his collections of pipes and antique walking sticks, his BMW, his six palaces, and his massive pantry full of caviar.

In fact, he was reputedly eating his favorite meal of caviar and trout when the bombs blew his world into tiny pieces. Had he anything left of himself to care, he would probably have mourned the most the loss of his massive set of records related to his international businesses and 95 billion dollars in bank accounts–not overseen by the Iranian Parliament–a figure much larger than the estimated wealth of the late hated Shah of Iran.

The second day in the battle of Iran, which could scarcely be recognized as such was more of a mopping up operation. It compared to the six-day war won by Israel in 1967 [known in the Arab world as "the set-back"] but would probably not last half that long. The American deep cover spies had drawn up maps of soft targets by the thousands—homes and headquarters of senior officers and government officials, administration buildings for mundane things like postal service, social welfare offices [such as they were], banks, and coastal customs operations. There was more pleasure—bittersweet at best, it can be granted—in destroying the infamous government prisons like Evin, located in Tehran—known by everyone in Iran as "hell on earth" and described by American Fox News network as "the home of many atrocities including widespread executions, tortures, and inhumane and unbearable conditions, especially for women". The destruction of the prisons was bittersweet for the Americans because they knew they were killing innocent victims within the prison walls; but in the long run, they were ridding the world of such ghastly hell-holes created by the Islamic Republic.

South Korean and British air forces joined in what became a crusade to destroy the rest of the hell holes besides Evin. They made hundreds of sorties to get rid of such places as Adel Abad Prison in Shiraz, Bandar Abbas Prison, in Hormozgan Province, the Central Prison of the Fashafoyeh neighborhood of Tehran, Ghezel Ghale Prison, all in Tehran, and Heshmatiyeh Prison just south of the capital city.

They worked into the night to destroy Dizel Abad Prison in Kermanshah, Falak-ol-Aflak Castle in Khorramabad, Gharchak Women's Prison, Ghezel Hesar Prison in Karaj, Karoun Prison in Ahvaz, and a host of others whose names became a blur; but their reputations drove the pilots on until exhaustion forced them to go to bed to rest up to go on with their work for another day. They felt as if they were the WWII soldiers who first discovered the Nazi concentration camps, and they had to rid the world of such evil.

It took another day to eradicate the infrastructure of the country's intelligence community, also known as a tool of the dictatorship and a source of unspeakable travesties committed against innocent people of *Iran*. The principle attacks centered on the Ministry of Intelligence, the Revolutionary Guards Intelligence, Police, and Military Intelligence Units–especially the Intelligence Security Unit of the Revolutionary Guard—which are the key intelligence services in the country. The Intelligence Agency–as a whole–was under the direct supervision of the Supreme Leader. The attackers particularly relished the idea of getting one more poke in the eye of Ali Khamenei, Supreme Leader of the Islamic Revolution.

In North Korea, there was one conspicuous failure. One American sortie sighted Kim Jong-un's very conspicuous airplane nearing the Yalu River Chinese border with his safety all but guaranteed in the PRC. It was an emotional and symbolic failure or even actual battle defeat, although it was of neither strategic nor a tactical importance. The little tyrant would likely gain refuge but would have to keep quiet if his stay in China and his continuing survival were to be assured. The American attackers encountered only sporadic defenses from North Korean air forces which spelled the doom for the defenders. Antiaircraft guns never hit a single American plane and were obliterated before the second hour of attack was finished.

Admiral Trescot ordered a leaflet barrage over the country on the third day after it appeared that all resistance by the North Korean military or ad hoc militias proved futile. The leaflets ordered all surviving citizens to bring their weapons and march to the coastal planes of Korea Bay where they would be confiscated. All survivors who complied would be given humane and all necessary medical treatment. All others would be hunted down as enemy combatants and "dealt with".

Trescot's second general order required two squadrons of hazmat teams to drive through the ruined cities to seek out survivors, particularly anyone capable of or intent on mounting counterattacks, however miniscule. The men and women of the hazmat forces drove about the area focusing infrared light spectrum thermal imaging at buildings and piles of rubble that could possibly be hiding places.

After forty-eight hours of a gridiron style search only 254 people were found. Ten of them attempted to fight and were summarily shot down; the rest were taken to the coast for treatment on the three naval hospital ships—the AH-6 *USS Comfort*, AH-7 *USS Hope*, and AH-8 *USS Mercy*—that had been brought to Korea Bay as hostilities commenced. The only bombing and strafing that had taken place at the prison camp sites concentrated on administration, torture, and troop buildings. The hazmat crews found that hardly any of the unfortunate political prisoners had been injured, and none killed.

The hazmat people—who looked like some sort of saviors from Mars to the traumatized survivors—were greeted with weeping, bowing, and shouting people who knew that they were experiencing a miracle. The miracle continued; every prisoner was taken by truck, bus, or ambulance, to the naval hospital ships.

A pitiful few weapons were confiscated by the victors. There were a few functional Chinese made automatic rifles, grenades, and only four machineguns, but there were old swords, WW II bayonets, hoes, picks, and hammers, taken from terrified former supporters of the regime and willing farmers. The two greatest accomplishments—besides the unconditional defeat and surrender of the rogue nation—for Admiral Trescot and his military, was that not a single American was killed or seriously injured. Two American sailors were bruised when they fell down ladders while hurrying to their posts when "All hands-on deck; man battle stations," was sounded. Only one artillery shot was fired from Pyongyang towards Seoul, and that one went awry. It was the least costly in terms of human expense of any American major military experience in history.

As the mop-up efforts progressed in the much larger country of Iran, the decimated nation yielded up only a total of 54,000 survivors, most of them in northern Kurdistan. Under interrogation, the vast majority of them turned out to have been long-time opponents of the Islamic State regime who were on Khamenei's most-wanted list. The walking wounded, burned, and the nonambulatory victims, were helped to US Army medical ships—which had been converted from other types ships in anticipation of the casualties in Iran and North Korea.

It could not be proved that the leadership of the IRI had been killed, but the complete lack of evidence for any survivors was taken as evidence enough that the cruel regime was finished. There was only one skirmish between Americans and a group of surviving Revolutionary Guards. The Guardsmen had surrendered and were in the process of stacking their arms while surrounded by hazmat suited SEALs and regular navy fighting men. The Guardsmen had been terrorized into abject submission by a loud-speaker system which preceded the American fighters playing *Hells Bells*.

I'm rolling thunder, pouring rain
I'm coming on like a hurricane
My lightning's flashing across the sky
You're only young but you're gonna die
I won't take no prisoners won't spare no lives
Nobody's putting up a fight
I got my bell I'm gonna take you to hell
I'm gonna get ya, satan get ya
Hells bells
Hells bells, you got me ringing
Hells bells, my temperature's high
Hells bells

Some fool fanatic revolutionary guard at the end of the line began firing wildly with his Russian made machine gun. Most of his ammunition simply went into the sky; the bullets that hit men killed and wounded only his fellow-guardsmen. But, the alarm was enough for the

SEALs and sailors to commence an orderly and careful crossfire that killed every guardsman remaining standing. The American LCDRs had no vehicles or inclination to haul corpses anywhere or to provide a decent burial; so, the dead were piled by bulldozers and a funeral pyre lit. The battle for Iran was finished.

CHAPTER
THIRTEEN

Fourteen sailors on the destroyer went on what would be a strike on civvie street, but on the Dragonfly and in the US Navy it was mutiny. The fourteen were buddies and were pretty much outsiders looking in according to shipmates. A previous president had declared homosexuals to be persona non grata and when discovered to be such were summarily booted out of the navy with a less than honorable rating whatever their career contributions had been. Four of the fourteen were somehow outed while they were at sea; the source of the incriminating evidence was unknown.

The other ten friends were outraged at the navy, at the ship's captain, and at the commander-in-chief, despite the fact that the first time she heard anything about it was on a "Breaking News" segment on Fox News. It would not have been news on CNN, had the fourteen not unitedly locked arms, sat down in the enlisted mess hall blocking the hatches, and refused to budge until their demands were met. The demands could not be ignored because the fourteen men went on a starvation strike and began to chant repeatedly and loudly,

"Justice for the LGBTQQIAAP in the US military, Justice for the LGBTQQIAAP in the military. We don't move until the president looks us in the face and agrees to change."

At first it was odd–then rather funny–but by the time it began to interfere with evening mess for the enlisted, it was a problem. No one particularly wanted to turn this into some big court marshal affair; so, the XO sent the ship's master-at-arms and his two deputies down the two ladders to the lower level of the destroyer to reason with them.

He said, "Listen you dumb shave heads, get up, get back to work, shut your mouths; and I won't have to learn your names. If I have to learn your names, that means paperwork; and I hate paperwork. On your feet. NOW!"

They said, "Justice for the LGBTQQIAAP in the US military, Justice for the LGBTQQIAAP in the military. We don't move until the president looks us in the face and agrees to change," and repeated endlessly until the CPO lost his cool.

"Shut up, what is this LGPQPOOP stuff anyway? At least talk sense. Give me a good reason to listen, or you will complete this deployment in the brig. Comprendo?"

The ring leader needed a little rest from the chanting; so, he patiently told the master-at-arms, "LGBT+ could be used for all of that as a short way to say the meaning of our community."

"Huh?" said the chief, "it's like you wuz speakin' Swahili to a pig."

"Hey, Chief, you know it's a way of spelling out our freedoms as Americans. L is for lesbian; G, for gay; B, for bisexual; T, for transsexual, the + stands for all the rest, which most people know, but we don't have to spell it all out."

"You can start with the T. What's that again?"

"People who accidently at birth were assigned the wrong sex. They see the world as the opposite of that they look like. A girl may look fully like a boy, but inside she understands herself to be a boy."

"Really, there's such a thing? What's in the rest of the +?"

"The next thing is Q,"

"What's that for?"

"Queer."

"Well, I get that. You mean there's more?"

"Yeah, I'll rattle the rest off for you. The whole thing is "LGBTQQIAAP. The second Q is for Questioning, the I stands for Intersex, the first A for Allies, the second A for Asexual, and the P is for Pansexual."

"You gotta be kiddin', is that stuff for real? I learned about boy and girl from my dad, and that was that in them days."

"Chief we have rights, including being left alone and not discriminated against anywhere, even on a navy ship."

The chief scratched his bald head.

"I'll get the doc."

Twenty minutes later, CDR Smithson arrived, had a polite chat, and repeated what the chief had said about them being arrested and put in the brig.

"You've made your point. Now quit all of this and save everybody a headache."

The problem was kicked its way up the stairs through the master of the ship, the XO, and finally to the captain.

He was brusque, "I am not talking to those guys, and neither are you. Get the master-at-arms to ask them politely one more time; and if they refuse, order them three times in a row. If they fail to obey, charge them with willful disobedience and tell them that I will see them at a Captain's Mast tomorrow morning."

"Aye, aye, Sir."

Half an hour later they were in the brig. In the captain's mast the following morning, the captain gave them one more chance.

The fourteen had hardened their stance, and now demanded to see the commander-in-chief as a condition to obey the captain's "illegal orders". One of the men had read somewhere that the famous woman president had once been the leader of the World Federation of Feminists; so, she had to be an arch liberal and a champion of causes like gay issues and especially of the plight of gays in the military.

After a long voyage spent in the cramped and uncomfortable accommodations in the brig, the fourteen men had become passionate mutineers and champions of their cause. The navy was not at all pleased with the idea that the press would get hold of their demand to see the president face-to-face. The desire by the JAG officers was to hold a general court marshal as soon as the destroyer made it into port.

CNO Dwight Halverson and SecNav Harold G. Neilsen had had their angst-ridden meeting two days before the *USS Dragonfly* made port in Norfolk. Under no circumstances were they going to allow this so-called "mutiny" to make a mockery out of the navy. The gay issue was a serious sore point with senior naval officers and had been ever since the populist right-winger had been president and had created havoc with his presidential anti-gay decree for the entire military. Now, it looked like the navy was going to face the gay issue in the press again and this time accompanied by a charge of mutiny. Mutinies just don't happen. Period.

When the CNO and SecNav left their meeting with President Daniels, she called in Presidential attorney Carter Anderton, White House attorney Lincoln Jukes, and Vice-president Frank Tatum. They had had a heads-up about the problem the day before and came prepared with specific information and recommendations.

Tatum was informally elected to explain.

"Madam President, I will jump down to the conclusion and recommendation. There have been two naval mutinies in our history, and they caused very considerable upheaval in the navy, in the country, and for the president at the time.

"The most recent and most definite occurred onboard the flagged US merchant ship *SS Columbia Eagle* in 1970 during the Vietnam war. Two crewmembers—members of the Seafarers International Union but called hippies by the other crew members–seized the vessel with the threat of a bomb and use of handgun and forced the master to sail to Cambodia. The vessel was a under contract to the government to take military napalm and explosives to US Thai air force bases to bomb Vietnam.

"The captain was forced to order 24 crew members to abandon the ship in lifeboats and sail the ship to the neutral nation of Cambodia. Once in Sihanoukville, the mutineers informed the government of Prince Norodom Sihanouk that they had seized the ship and its cargo as an act of protest and claimed asylum as anti-war Marxist revolutionaries. Unfortunately for them, Cambodia had just started a civil war which led to the rise of the pro-American Khmer Republic.

The mutineers became prisoners of Prime Minister Lon Nol's right-leaning government. One of them gave up and served a prison sentence for mutiny, kidnapping, assault, and neglect of duty, and served his sentence. The other escaped from Cambodian custody along with a US army deserter, and the two fled north hoping to join the state-communist Khmer Rouge as freedom fighters but were executed by the guerrillas in 1971. It would be an extreme understatement to say that the president's favorability rating plummeted.

"The second 'mutiny' is the better example for you to consider when making your decision because it involved black people, and a miscarriage of justice. Just insert gays instead of blacks, and you have the defense's position in the legal proceedings that may come.

"I'll be brief about what led up to the charges of mutiny being filed by the navy. One July, 7, 1942, African-American stevedores working in the Port of Chicago were loading the *USS Bryan*, a navy ship, when it blew apart taking out everything in an 800 yard radius, including another ship and several buildings. 320 people in the ships or working on the dock were killed and 390 badly injured. Only fifty-one of the dead could be identified. A huge fireball rose into the night sky and mushroomed nearly three miles across, throwing fiery debris as high as 12,000 feet.

"A navy investigation revealed that the *Bryan* had 1,552 tons of high explosives stowed in its several holds, and another 200 tons waiting to be loaded on the dock. All but five of the victims, were right on top of the explosion. The officers in charge of the stevedores–all of whom were white–were granted a month's leave to recover and recuperate; but their black subordinates were kept in quarters and not allowed time away. All suffered severe emotional trauma. The black men were put back to work as soon as workspaces became available.

"Now, here is where the mutiny comes in. On Aug. 8, 1944, the ammo carrier *Sangay* tied up across from Port Chicago, and African-American stevedores were ordered to prepare to load the ammunition. The officer in charge of one of the loading divisions informed the commander of the Vallejo Naval Barracks that most of his men were refusing–out of fear–to report to work as ordered. The senior officer at the port told the sailors individually that their continued refusal to obey orders would necessitate disciplinary action. Some men in other labor divisions also refused to work, and some sailors said they would readily obey any order except one that involved handling ammunition. In all, 258 men from three separate labor divisions declared their intention not to engage in any form of the work involving ammunition.

"The sailors who refused to report for work were separated from their units and placed in a group. The admiral in charge told them about the critical need for ammunition to reach units then fighting on Saipan, appealed to their sense of duty, and told them plainly that their refusal to return to their primary duty of loading munitions amounted to an act of mutiny. He warned them that mutiny in time of war was a crime punishable by death.

"Most of the black sailors had assumed that mutiny only applied in cases where a crew attempted to seize control of a vessel; they had no such intention. When the order to report for ammunition loading was repeated, 208 men reluctantly fell in, but 50 others still refused, and were immediately confined in the brig at Camp Shoemaker.

"The JAG officer assigned to their defense determined that none of the enlisted men knew the official definition of mutiny, which–according to Section 46 of the Naval Courts and Boards–is 'the unlawful opposition or resistance to or defiance of superior military authority, with deliberate purpose to usurp, subvert, or override such authority.' That, Madam President, applies in the present case. The navy then began the process that would result in the largest court-martial for mutiny in its history which convened in September, 1944.

"The defendants were divided into five groups of 10 each, with one attorney for each group. The defense argued that because the accused sailors had acted only out of fear, and not from any "deliberate purpose to usurp, subvert, or override, superior military authority," the legal standard required to prove mutiny had not been established.

"The prosecution countered that all that was necessary to prove that a mutiny occurred was to show that the men in question refused to "perform military service" after they were given the order and then warned of the consequences of disobedience. The prosecutor added that the willful disobedience at Port Chicago was 'an extraordinary case of conspiracy … [and] of mutiny.'

"The seven officers who made up the court deliberated for less than 90 minutes, then found all 50 defendants guilty. Each was sentenced to 15 years in prison and dishonorable discharge.

"The admiral reduced the sentences of 40 of the sailors to prison terms ranging from eight to 12 years. The 206 men who had initially disobeyed the order to work but relented after being threatened with the charge of mutiny had all been tried on charges of refusing to obey a lawful order and received lesser sentences.

"The idea that a mutiny occurred on a naval ship did not sit well with the brass or the president. So, six days after the court-martial adjourned, a Navy court of inquiry investigated and found:

A general failure to foresee and prepare for the tremendous increase in explosives shipments as the critical need for steady ammunition resupply to the Pacific Theater grew; so, safety took a lesser position than speed.

A failure to provide an adequate number of competent petty officers or even personnel of petty officer caliber.

The navy deprived the stevedores of capable supervision at the first-line level. As a result, the lack of African-American petty officers meant that the sailors in the racially segregated labor units had no authority figures to advocate on their behalf.

Port Chicago was crewed by junior officers—all of them white, and none of them had the requisite experience in directly supervising enlisted men and no training in the handling and loading of munitions.

There was inadequate training at all levels, and that was evident from reports coming from port operations from the beginning of the war.

The investigative board faulted the command climate at Port Chicago for failing to provide facilities that could have boosted the morale of the enlisted men as they carried out their dangerous, exhausting work. The investigators were willing to state that the faults were due to the policy of racial segregation practiced by the navy.

The court of inquiry argued that the morale problems were not a consequence of poor training or treatment. They went on to state that the enlisted men were "unreliable, emotional, lacked capacity to understand or remember orders or instructions, were particularly susceptible to mass psychology and moods, lacked mechanical aptitude, were suspicious of strange officers, disliked receiving orders of any kind, particularly from white officers or petty officers, and were inclined to look for and make an issue of discrimination.

"Later investigation determined that such characterizations were completely unfair. The fact that the stevedore units were exclusively black, without black officers or petty officers, created an environment of outright discrimination and racial tension. Nonetheless, the Navy insisted that the black ordnance units 'were administered and trained in the same manner as all other enlisted men in the Navy.' Upon review, that proved to be false. The court martial was reopened by the navy—even to the public and the press to quiet criticism for its prior dealings with the black mutineers.

"In response to the offer, the NAACP sent Thurgood Marshall–a young lawyer who would one day sit on the U.S. Supreme Court–to California to observe the trials. Not surprisingly, Marshall found the court-martial and its verdicts inherently unfair. He drafted an appeal for the Judge Advocate General of the Navy in which he noted that both prosecution and defense had used the same sources of legal authority to argue their respective positions on the mutiny question, and he underscored the obvious flaw in the charge — 'there is no set rule as to what is mutiny.' Furthermore, it was outrageous that the court had deliberated for so short a time before convicting 50 men and consigning them to prison and dishonorable discharge in violation of the constitutional right to a speedy trial. He also argued that the navy's practices regarding African-Americans were inherently unequal, and therefore, unjust.

"There was a hew and cry around the country which—along with Marshal's pertinent legal points–yielded results, one of which was significant, even though Marshall lost his appeal.

The Navy began to reconsider both its ammunition handling protocols and its racial segregation practices.

The Navy ordered the sentences of the Port Chicago 50 reduced by one year.

Public pressure mounted; the president was beset by critics, especially by the growing number of anti-segregationists and those opposed to the unequal rights being endured by African-Americans.

Finally, in January, 1946, 47 of the 50 men were released and paroled to active service at sea. Those who incurred no further disciplinary actions were finally discharged from the Navy 'under honorable conditions.'

Mutiny got redefined.

"The 'mutiny' case was important in the long climb uphill to genuine equal treatment. The controversy over the Port Chicago court-martial continued to resonate in legal and political forums for the next 60 years. By the 1990s, journalists and historians came to describe the incident at Port Chicago as a 'work stoppage' or 'strike,' overlooking the fact that such distinctions do not exist in the military. That change has cemented in the minds of liberal thinking people—perhaps the Silent Majority— that the case and the treatment of those stevedores was a travesty, and the Navy had to be dragged kicking and screaming into the light of the new era of racial equality and justice. Incidentally, most of the former sailors never even sought presidential pardons. Pardons were for the guilty, and to the very end they insisted they were innocent of the crime for which they had been imprisoned.

"Now, Madam President, what do you propose to do about the newer, but very similar injustice?"

"Oh, good grief, what do you two think, Carter, Lincoln? I might as well tell you that VP Tatum is in good company with the CNO and the Sec/Nav."

"To pursue this is like Cleopatra putting her hand into a basket full of asps," Lincoln said.

"This is a lose-lose arrangement, Madam President," Carter told her. "I think you should quit while you're ahead."

"All right, I'll get the order drawn up. We'll let the charges drop, assign all of the men to different ships, and quietly tell them that the president has already started to dismantle the policy of discrimination of the LGBTQ. I would just as soon the White House not be quoted about the mutiny charge; that is just lifting up a rock to reveal the crawlephants underneath with nothing to gain. Make it public that the White House is going to reverse its policy again and leave the gays alone.

"However, the nation has not heard the last of this. I will work to correct this evil unworthy of the United States, and one day I will be in a position where I can say what I want to say and do what should be done; and the critics will not be able to prevent me from doing the nation's work for doing so.

"Abraham Lincoln, in a speech given in New Haven, Connecticut in 1860 said it very well, 'Neither let us be slandered from our duty by false accusations against us, nor frightened from it by menaces of destruction to the government, not of dungeons to ourselves. Let us have faith that right makes might; and in that faith, let us, to the end, dare to do our duty, as we understand it.'"

"He was a better man than me, but my time will come; and I will right this wrong, so help me, God."

EPILOGUE

Sybil Norcroft Daniels survived forty-seven years after the end of her presidency. She outlived her husband, Charles, by twenty-five years, her daughter, Cerisse, by ten years, and her granddaughter by five.

She served as the Dean of the Harvard Medical School for five years and as president of the university for twenty-two years after that. She was 112 years old when she died, and she would have lived to a ripe old age but for a freak accident that occurred while she was learning how to parasail.

Kim Jong-un lived to be sixty-two and died in a medium grade nursing home in Wuhan, China having never again held any political or military office. He was a ward of the Chinese state with considerable limitations on his ability to travel. His sister, Kim Yo Jong, took over the reins of government in what was left of North Korea, but there were not enough people surviving to need any form of government. She died at the age of forty-five of leukemia. A few nomadic Asian wanderers moved in and out of the north without founding any permanent towns. The region that was once North Korea, became a desert, almost devoid of plants or animals.

The region that was once Persia and later Iran was a barren wasteland into which even hazmat-clad scientists dared not enter. There were no more than 100 acres of arable, nuclear free land in the area once occupied by a great and powerful nation on the fiftieth anniversary of the nuclear attack.

The nations around the arid desert forgot about her; she was erased from history. Also, around her, Sunni Muslims prospered, fought, had attempts at becoming Islamic States, and generally carried on their preferred form of life. Shi'a Muslims were no longer seen in the Middle East, but a few small communities held on in Europe and South America. In the 2060 census in America, there were less than fifty people who claimed to be Shi'a Muslims.

The United States of America in 2055 was a runt of its former self. The remaining territory which had legal ownership of the name included the former Middle Western and Rocky Mountain States. What had been the continental United States was divided into seven irregularly shaped entities that had split from the rest because of racial, ideological, religious, political, and irreconcilable economic, differences. Alaska, Hawaii, Guam, and Puerto Rico, all went their separate ways. None of the current entities of the former USA ranked in the top thirty-five largest among global economies, militaries, or populations.

China patiently waited its turn to be the biggest, greatest, and most powerful, nation followed by Brazil/Argentina, Germany, the Union of France, England, the Netherlands, and Ireland forming what they called The European Union of States. All the other countries in the European continent went their separate ways content to be small, happy, and simple, neutral countries freed from the endless round of hostilities, prejudices, and ambitions, of the previous countries and the present-day entities that were still striving.

-THE END-